STREET GAMES

takes us into the world of George Street, Brooklyn, where all kinds of people cope with the ups and downs of life.

Meet Luis, whose grocery store attracts more burglars than customers. Cecil, the landlord, who cares for his troubled sister. Margaret, the mother of a "special" child. Ismael the junkie and Naomi the shoplifter. And many others— happy and sad, but always colorful, as they grapple with the many challenges of life.

STREET GAMES

Also by Rosellen Brown
Published by Ballantine Books

TENDER MERCIES

AUTOBIOGRAPHY OF MY MOTHER

STREET GAMES

ROSELLEN BROWN

BALLANTINE BOOKS • NEW YORK

for my mother and father

"A Letter to Ismael in the Grave" was one of the *O. Henry Prize Stories for 1972*, and "Mainlanders," which does not appear here intact but was the source for at least four of these stories, not to mention the spirit of the whole, is published in the *O. Henry Prize Stories for 1973*.

I am immensely grateful to the George and Eliza Howard Foundation for their grant for the years 1971–72.

CONTENTS

268 George Street

(corner Leon)

I AM NOT LUIS BEECH-NUT

How long it take you to go all around the world? A day
and a half something like that? A day and a half I get
up, drink this Bustelo down with grit in the bottom,
dirt, and I tell Adela get another sleeve for the coffee,
this little flannel for the cup, this one is stinking by
now and have a hole. I'm looking at the Bustelo bag,
the yellow always look so old and faded, and in my
mind I got to learn these things, it's true it say
"TOSTADO Y ENVASADO POR BUSTELO COFFEE
ROASTING CO. (Div. of Beech-Nut, Inc.)" Son of a
bitch. "Tostado y Molido Para El Gusto Hispano"—y
el Profit Americano. Like me. Their little fertilizer,
manure, what you call it, for their flower gardens, beauty
roses. Little shit, this Luis, and all day long George
Street, Leon Street, going by the store so fast you think
I'm selling the plague in here two for a dollar.

No, I was saying what I do while the world going
round, and I could go with it—if I was Luis Beech-
Nut. I drink this shit down, wipe my mouth, push my
mustache out flat, scatter the crumbs for the birds,
buckle up my belt that I keep loose for breakfast, and
goodby, seven days a week. The girls, some of them
are up, Enery go on sleeping, she'll be sleeping when
the last day of the great world come, and I go on.
Adela come later, all the help she bring me. Whatever
a woman is good for might be between the sheets she
wash—Adela will do, I'm not a man who force a
woman to be *una puta*, you know—but this one of
mine, she is mostly a maker of girl children to embar-
rass me. Not one boy in that lot, just all these babies
with those little bottoms that are always cloved like the
devil's feet. I checked each time I had one of them

3

alone the first time, put my hands in the diaper, hoping
for a mistake, something to get hold of, but the only
sticks in this family, Jesús, are the one of mine and the
one that prop the kitchen window open in the summer!

And then after making herself round with kids in
front before, and behind after, she is a first-class maker
of mistakes at the store. The adding machine is like
some mystery, it could be a rocket ship, she stand there
with her fingers on the controls, they could be her feet
in shoes, not graceful, and smile her little smile looking so scared, and drive away the customers right into
the arms of Anthony and his thieves' market up there.
So I tell her to scrub the counter while I go up to the
money, eleven cents for one can of tomato sauce—tell
me what can you do with one can?—and she polish
and shine, that metal edge on the counter is like a
mirror, till she deserve a genie popping out of it, and
say: Lady, what your wish? I don't know about her but
my wish is two dozen ladies coming in to do the whole
week's shopping one after another, they say No More
Supermarkets, Never, with their big squeaky carts parked
over there in the corner. Asking for staples first, economy size, and then all the stupid little things that last
sucker, *coño*, had to go and order. What for? Capers?
How many capers you think I sell in a week? Chili yes,
cumino, but what is this other stuff here. This lemon-
pepper, marjoram, coriander? This was never any
Gristedes, not even the old days. No wonder that old
Jew sold out.

So. This morning. I have seen the old McTave lady
who buy Alka-Seltzer so often she going to take off
her roof some morning and never stop, fly out to sea.
Seventy-three cents, plus tax on the Alka-Seltzer.
Fontaine over there come get himself an electric-green
toothbrush. He brush in the dark? Then from across
the intersection, long distance, that slut, that nigger
girl who hustle for the *tecato*, what she come for?
Adela watch me with her eyes little when she twitch
her ass at me, but it's O.K., I don't like women that
are built like tweezers. I swear to the Virgin Mary, she
heap up a little pile and give me her business dimple:
one box kitchen matches, one small can Hormel corned
beef hash, panty-hose on sale, cloud-mist, two for $1.07,

and a pack of gum. The matches go for his habit, the stockings go for hers, the dog eat the corned beef, I bet you, and they all split the gum. What else I got to do here but think?

I rearranged everything on the shelves twice already, I'm trying ways to get your eye when you walk in—if nobody's around I pretend to come in the door and what hit me? Campbell's Pork and Beans. O.K., now what would go good with it to put by its right hand? You got to strain yourself to do this, what they call good retailing practices. Bread and butter pickles. I try that for a day. The label's getting this dust that stick, damp dust, I'm afraid to go see what the basement doing to me, but I can't dust it off and I can't wash it. At the door when I'm pretending to come on in smiling, pocket full of change and no holes in it, the cod stink and the whole place have such dust flying in on the light it could be a barnyard back home with a cockfight going on.

I don't know. Eight years' work at Cappy's Market, two months here, my Grand Opening banners are still out there looking like a lord's funeral, and that Jew that bought me all that coriander went to where? Palm Springs? Palm Beach? Someplace warm, a little closer to my Bayamón, no seven-day-a-week nightmares, and gave it all to Luis instead, and after my last breakfast of steamed shit they going to bury me under the concrete out back if things don't shake out better soon. I can add, my machine can add if my wife stay off it, but all I get to add is OUTGOING, cash, credit. Everything else is *subtracción*.

I take a candle home. Adela will say shame but she be the first to help me light it. The candles are selling better because what's her name, that Hortensia, old Negri, down George corner of Smith, dropped dead a couple weeks ago with a goiter as big as that mailman's pouch out there. So her Botánica is shut up behind a ripped old black shade. How could she die, and screaming, they said, like a saint sent to hell by mistake, with all the herbs and candles and little sacks of cures right there? Well, she died sure as she lived, sitting there in that old couch popping springs, telling people how to change Jesus's mind or get their mans back, his wandering ass back in their bed, if you'll pardon me. She brought luck with the horses, luck with the *boleta*. Tony Aguilar said it was rat-shit but she did him a good turn, he won three hundred dollars the day before her goiter choked her. Luck with women who couldn't bear—not so much luck with the ones who bore stones they didn't want to carry, I can promise you that—but she died.

And I got her business. The nearest spirit woman now, it make you think, is a bus ride, thirty-five cents, or that blind woman up State Street who only do bad spells, death, or make sworn enemies disappear. And the nearest *bodega* that gots candles is a good solid walk. Nobody want to go a block rain or shine these days, you notice? We getting like the suburbs, only with rats and no parking. Anthony's little shelf shits but he don't need that business, when he sell one out, say St. Michael, it stay out till the person who need it fall down dead or go broke. Can they sue him for lousy inventory? So there's the PEACEFUL HOME candle, and the MONEY DRAWING that has to say (ALLEGED) in small letters we all so honest now, while Beech-Nut take all the money away in a wheel-barrow anyhow. SAFE CROSSING sell in going-home season, the 7 AFRICAN POWERS so-so, the WORK candle, all the saints, and the black ones with no words and a cat hissing with his back arched way up.

Maybe somebody gots one burning for me. Hey that's a good idea. Trying to get me on the welfares. Two packs of cigarettes. Adela sell them and what can she mess up? She forget the matches. The blond bitch come on back in and ask for them making these little lips to tell us she's pissed off for the ten extra steps. I hold out a handful and she take two. The cat bring a mouse up the cellar stairs and drop it splat right in front of the bread rack. Stiff already. Some kid, Widdoes his name is, come over from the Projects, and I hate it but I tell him go home and tell your mama no, no more credit, not till I get that page full of hot dog dinners paid back here. Enough. It's enough this place eat up my bank account, do they mean to pull my hairs out one by one?

I went home last night, my Enery, my first best daughter I had when I was nineteen and had the best still in me, she is waiting to ask a question. What, dear? I got a problem, from school. What, you got in some trouble? No. She is almost blond, bless her, we call her Blanqui, I don't know where she get that but she always like a movie starlet with that wavy hair that give off lights like a three-way bulb. No, I mean some homework, I don't know what to do with it. She bring her notebook that's fat with doodlings of girls with all their noses pointed up. It say on the blue line:

LIST 5 REASONS BEHIND MAN'S DESIRE TO ESCAPE THIS WORLD.

This is for what class?

She don't remember that, only she going to have to answer it somehow. I say, what you think, Dolly? My name for this beautiful girl. Blanqui, you can do this.

Well, love? Maybe sometimes love goes wrong? She is thinking of her soldier who took her little silver ring off to Vietnam and she worry will they let him wear it? They took all his hair away, maybe they get his ring too. She going to get married when he come back (if, I say, but never to her) and he get his army pay and then her sweet cherry she been saving, and her baby-sitting bank account too, and don't laugh, one of these days I wake up and see it bigger than mine. All those half-babies of hers get to wait a little longer where it's warm inside her while the other half run away from flying bullets.

Yes, I say. Love.

And there's always war.

War. Sure, war.

She bite her finger-knuckle thinking. Maybe they're afraid to die. I tell her write that. That's good. They can't escape but they want to if they could. She print it out slowly and carefully. Her writing go both ways, left, right, and straight up. That's three. Sickness, that's not the same as dying. *Sí.* Write it. Pain and sickness, you could say. Sometimes it take forever just to die.

Now she is out of griefs. Imagine that, to be seventeen. Enery, *mi vida*, I say, and I take her hands. Enery, think hard.

She make big eyes at me, looking into mine. Little stranger who already outgrew all the Spanish she ever want to know, who is so smart in the dress department, and polished fingernails, and pants. *Muchacha*, money. You ever heard of money? *El dinero?* What make the whole world go around? And is killing your father? (I don't say that. Why make her wounds for me to bleed from?) She looking a little disappointed—oh that— but she still need one more or she get a bad grade, so she write in MONY and smile and slam her book closed, gone already halfway down the stairs to meet her friends. I watch them from the window going around to the church to play or up to Livingston, Fulton, the stores to spend her baby-sitting money? To go put her little nose, that don't turn up like her pictures, right against the dusty window at the *joyería*, she make eyes at this ring, fifty-eight carats or fifty-eight facets or what, she want her boy to buy her so bad she pay half herself. Why? I'm smart now. So they can get married and be in hock already on their wedding night to a man who hack up stones and sell the chips and dust? Then to the furniture man? Then everything, and sure to be a baby hatching by the time the sun come up. I don't want her eyes wet but once in a while I see a bullet keeping him there forever, a nice boy, decent, but so she remember the best of him, what they planned, not what the whole world gots planned for them.

Three times I left Adela or she left me, one time she had a good cut across her eye that left a scar, once a slash I won't say where, with a Gem, the usual thing. The first time Enery was just walking, then a couple more times, don't ask me why I went, why I came back like a tomcat bleeding between the legs. I feel like I grow up since then, or I don't care about some things as much as others no more. I mind my business. I only want to say, I wish my Enery could stay just like she is this minute, no matter what she doing: bending over to tie her shoe that's in style right up to the second, this year lacing shoes, like they always going out hiking, last year platforms, they up on the third floor just walking down the block, laughing, her teeth so perfect and white like baby teeth, and her skirt pulling up in back over these strong legs Adela never had with her tree-stumps. Looking like a girl who can go home to a comfortable bed and no sisters in it, no men, no tears in it, not real tears she bleed from her womb, or her little breasts like milk. No standing on line at the prison door with packages, no running to the hospital, Jesús, no doing foul things standing up in the stair wells like her father done. *Mi Blanquita*, who give me one more reason not to close the gates to this beat-down store for the last time and run someplace before the creditors come up behind me with blackjacks.

But. One more thing to tell about Rojas Spanish Favorites. It should have been born a pool hall. The one robbery don't matter much, it was only an insult because I knew this *maricón* who come bouncing in here with his finger poking in his pocket like a hard-on, he called it a *gun*. "Hey, spic, I got a *gun* here. No tricks." Was he on the late show? O.K., you know what he went home with, back down to Baltic Street where he live with his mamma? Eleven dollars, one check I wasn't so sure was worth a piss against the wall, two unopen packages, one dimes, one pennies— see, I let him take it all out of the money box himself. He'd of killed me if I gave that and say that's all. He had to come *see*. So he shovel it into his pocket, he still fierce, his cheeks going, his eyes bugged, and he can't smile or laugh at the little turds I get to call my profit. His profit now! Can't spare a smile. I can't even make change, man—these big executive bastards, whatever they are, they come in on the way home from the subway with their tens, their twenties for a pack of Larks, a quart of milk and I get wiped out, no change, I got to let them go. Right out of the net up to Anthony's or do without milk. So this bandit, he can't let up and laugh because we both getting the same pitchfork shook at both of us, he just go clomp, clomp, out, no more gun, and slam the door I keep propped open to be inviting. The bells jangle and I laugh till these giant tears come out and wash the scared shitless sweat right off my face. And you know what I'm thinking—just the luck, Luis, you could get your head blown off for eleven bucks too. For eleven cents.

But what I start to say. The only real trouble I had in here besides cream going bad and the offers on the box top expiring before some kid get his hands on them, and me drying up like 120 pounds of salt cod?—it was a time about a week ago some *chulo*, this pimp, come

walking in here. Yeah, I'm remembering when I used
to look at shoes like that, and suits—good I didn't see
his car, the pain used to get me in the groin like a bite
with all the teeth closed, when I was younger. As soon
as I saw him I knew he had big trouble in his fist. He
was a wop who tried some Spanish on me. But I didn't
like that, I shook it off and asked him in English what
he want. I felt, I tell you, like a whore some customer
was trying to kiss, you know? Just close the door behind
you and get the fucking over with. What you want,
amigo? Some fruit juice, what you got? Tomato, prune,
orange, orange-grapefruit, some of it's in the refrigerator, nice and cool. And, let's see, maybe a small
bottle of grape. Right. Welch's. The best. Got any
pineapple? All out. Sorry. Just sold the last can. (Adela
took it home yesterday to drink herself. I got to watch
that.) So he take this midget grapefruit juice and look
all around, slow. Oh, and spaghetti-o's. For lunch, he
tell me. What, he going to open the can with his teeth?
    So this dago pimp talk a little. About how much
noise and dirt the bus make, where does it go? George
Street, this is a major thoroughfare? I laugh. Yeah,
everybody go by so fast they can't stop themself. But
they wave when they go by. No really. *Sí*, really. You
want a good burial plot? I'm trying to discourage him,
get him to not notice me. More, nonsense, this bubble-
gum talk. I want to ask him what's the point. I mean,
he don't want to buy me out. He walk around on the
balls of his fifty-buck shoes while little Luz Pacheco
buy a dime worth of candy penny by penny, thinking
hard. I wasn't so sure I'd live long enough to hear what
he want. Finally. I could guess. A little trouble with
Anthony up there, the bodega where everything hot
except for the grocery business. He didn't say that but
it's clear. Something he wasn't doing that they wanted.
Did I ever put a little money down on a number? *Ay*,
who doesn't? What would I think of using this place
for, you know, a drop? I could use a little business,
no? And maybe a little consideration, one kind or
another? Something nice to keep the warm juices flow-
ing? This was a man not much bigger than me but
broad in the shoulders, broad maybe only with a shoulder holster, how do you know? What do I see? Blood,

of course—Anthony's, mine, Adela in the middle of some cross fire, the traffic ticket cops dropping their books and coming in with their guns out. Also I see myself wearing some shirts I like, maybe, not this worn-out dishrag because I won't keep more than rent and lights and school clothes for the kids out, all the rest of nothing stay in inventory. I want to go home and go to sleep, that's all. I'm young but not that young. People I know go around wishing they could make this kind of connections and I'm just standing here. But it's not the dirty part that scaring me, breaking the law, I mean we a people who gots our own law, the law down Court Street don't do much for me, give it all to the men with their feet up on their shiny desk. The part that scare me is all the rest. This connection put your clean face right up against an asshole that never get wiped. You know? Like you get involved you disappear down this long tunnel, who know where you come out, or how. And you can't call nobody for help, who you call?

See, I never was strong about much, just hung on. I just say this, I say so much already. All my life I got this little problem with women. With myself, I mean. I can get it up, no trouble, I always can, first thing, long before I see the bull's-eye in front of me, but only once. Can't hit a double, you could say, a triple, go all the bases, a grand slam. One time at a time. O.K.? No complaints. Well, this is it, the store. My one time. This is it for the rest of my whole life, and I admitted the first week when I totaled up it's a lousy lay, too—numb. Nothing. Is this what I been saving all these years for? Going without? But you never want it to stop, do you, anyway? You don't want to be all done with it and no more coming.

So I told him O.K. Fine. We get the guarantees straightened out, I say no hot goods in here, I don't want nobody's ripped-off televisions, no drugs, nothing like that. Sure, *amigo*. He pat my back. I'm not wearing his kind of sharkskin. We shake hands. Whose guarantees? These *chulos*, they can move around, go where they want, get out when the wind change, and here I am with my banners and my light bill and yesterday's potato salad. Luis Beech-Nut, he could sweep these bastards out with his broom, throw the cat at them, call the cops, say no blood on my floor, you listening, unless it's yours.

But I got to say maybe they'll be some new faces in here with their quarters, new friends, new half-dollars with some new president on them. Maybe I should have asked for time to think but I got this feeling they don't do that kind of business. Pay now, think later. Well, I don't got to make it gangster paradise in here, I can keep the place alive like Anthony never did, still selling two-year-old Ivory Snow that look like a car came in his window and ran over the box. If he don't come down here and kill me first.

So here I am. A couple more sales, they saying it take time, all the time take time. I'm taking my pail and go put suds in the water, wash down the sidewalk, the least I can do. Otherwise it all pile up out there and I see enough dust inside all day. George Street, you and your hurry, you looked so good to me when I came to see this place. Back and forth like the ocean tides, all these well-dressed people who look like they eat good, smoke a lot, drink a six-pack every night, and this corner is a little pebble sticking up in the tide. How was I supposed to know nothing stop here? Nothing except the cars for the stop sign, not even a mailbox, a trash can, nothing. I got a sign out there that say NO PARKING, M–F, 7–11, 4–7. Big shit. Listen to Luis, goddamn. Goddamn, I'm cutting the price of milk today. Two cents, running a risk. *Mira!* Will you come in now?

261

(lower duplex)

THE ONLY WAY TO MAKE IT IN NEW YORK

She had caught him going through her jewelry. She stood on the threshold in her slick raincoat, balancing on her toes, looking casual, almost, as though she were coming in to tell him, "Dinner is served." It was faintly amusing—he would pick up a necklace, hold it toward the ceiling light critically, then fling it down. She was embarrassed, it was like being in an accident and worrying in the ambulance about your dirty underwear. There was so little there, only a ring or two of sentimental value, if that. (Grandma gave her a sapphire at graduation, but Grandma was a shrew in Palm Beach who had chewed her mouth away—or so it had always looked—and had sharpened her voice till it was a pointed stick to skewer the world with. When she'd been eighteen and stayed out late, Grandma had taken to calling her "Chippie," so what was her ring supposed to be worth?) Oh—Martin's watch with the good expanding band. Into his lumpy pocket it went. Her good pearls were hanging out like a dirty hanky.

She was waiting to be frightened. But she wouldn't be. He had no gun that she could see. He was not the man she was expecting, anyway, so she was not about to be intimidated. In fact he was pathetic by comparison. That was funny enough to make her smile and she was sure he would turn around at that; the mock-bitter movement of her lips had sent a million hairline cracks through the air as though it were ice.

She'd been sure, after the first robbery, that it was Tony Aguilar's brother-in-law. Together he and Tony had been building closets and a room divider between the front bedroom and Wendy's little L. The lousy

15

apartment with its painted-over marble fireplaces (styles change but then, dammit, they change back again and you're left with a gallon of paint stripper. She tended to think of it as a fifty-buck-a-month place. Too bad the landlord didn't). Tony was a wide, brown, rough, sweet man with miles of kinky hair, raised around the corner and making good, good enough, with his carpentry. He was a daddy, and respected. His wife's brother was a junkie. Willie came to work and took off his shirt first thing, showing muscles that made her stomach sink. It was a disgusting reaction, adolescent, but she couldn't help it. He had a clean face, sharply cut, Aztec, with a distant vulnerability in the eyes which could only have been the drugs. Something about him was like cream, maple cream, incredibly inviting to touch, where it dipped and flowed over his shoulder blades as he hammered boards inexpertly. She got out fast, later to work each day: she saw his back all the way to the subway. She'd have thought a junkie would look unhealthy. Martin, seamy and mustard-yellow under his tee shirt, looked unhealthy.

Well, the junkie didn't look good when he came around at dinnertime, worse at two in the morning, banging angrily as though they ought to have been expecting him. Money, money, just an advance against more nailing, more sawing so they would have closets for their nice nice clothes. Lady listen. My grandmother, I need it. Near tears, those eyes racing all around ready for escape, his knuckles white, fingertips biting palms cruelly. Martin had asked why Tony couldn't help, or his sister. There was a muttered reply. From where she lay, Martin looked like the heavy. He breathed hard in his maroon robe, laboring at saying no, making it a whole moral business, who cared, who wanted speeches, explanations, truth? Martin was always giving quarters to beggars on the street after he'd extracted the name of the wine they were going to spend it on. A quarter was cheap for that song and dance. He came back to bed shaking his head.

"Don't you think he wanted a fix?" She had lit a cigarette and pushed the smoke out with the force of her irritation.

"Well, I wasn't going to let him have it."

"What will he do?"

"Do you really want to concern yourself with that? What do you care what a dope addict does? He must have friends in some alley somewhere. Let him get his assistance elsewhere."

He took off his robe and sat on the edge of the bed, looking perplexed, his pale flesh gathering in dewlaps around his middle. They were so deep there was true shadow under them, she thought idly. Can you hold a pencil under your breasts? Under your flaps of fat, my dear, can you hold a candle.

Tony's brother came back the next two nights, banging and threatening, but apologetic when they opened the door, as though passion had unmanned him, then let him go. He was a small animal, a ferret, in the mouth of a predator, and one of these days it wasn't going to spit him out alive. Then he stopped coming. But at the end of the week they let themselves in after a party and found all their electrical appliances gone. Wendy had been staying with a friend that night or she'd have been home alone; this was her first season baby-sitting herself.

She had walked around picking things up and dropping them. She felt strangely like a mother cat—no, what animal was it? A mouse?—that loses interest in its babies once they've been handled by someone else. Her underwear, Martin's, lying in a twisted heap, was dishonored, as if by a voyeur. Books lay in a blasted mountain where they'd been tipped off the mantel. Her one poor fur was gone, an antique muskrat that would get the thief a dollar on a good day. The silver was still there—she opened and closed the drawer with astonishing indifference; none of the details mattered much. All the cupboard doors were open in the kitchen and there was one mug, soiled at the lip, in the middle of the floor, a rootbeer bottle tipped over beside it. She picked it up gingerly as if by the tail and dropped it in the wastebasket. The mail drawer was rifled, letters perhaps read. She felt incredibly dirty, but that was all. It came as a shock to realize that she cared not one little bit about what had been taken.

The question then was, reporting to the police, should they implicate Aguilar's wife's brother? Willie—

whatever his name was. He could have made a key so easily, both of them out all day, Wendy in school. How much trust it took to get through a single day in the world. . . . But she felt queasy about that, on what she called "moral grounds." Martin, angry, dismissed morality.

"Your grandiloquence could find a better cause. I don't want to get sued for false arrest. Accusation. Whatever the hell it is."

"Oh, he'd never *sue* you."

"Who knows what he'd do, a desperate man?" Martin had been going around making an inventory of their losses for his tax return. He seemed mildly elated by the coincidence that would bring them next year's models of solid-state this and automatic-refraction-tuning that, with a tax write-off at current resale values.

"The hundred dollars deductible is deplorable," he was saying—he said it three times—while she picked up a pair of pantyhose that was twined around the bodice of a slip, saw a greasy fingerprint on the daisy embroidery, and dropped it again.

"Who are you?" was all she could think to say now, stupid as it sounded. He was compact, dark, dirty, and concentrating hard on the pathetic cache of jewelry like a competent workman puzzling over shoddy goods.

She was still in the doorway. She could run, she had calculated, if he turned on her. But she didn't think he would.

He looked at her levelly.

"Who are you?"

"Why do you want to know my name? I just took a couple of your rings, that's all you got to know, right?"

He was wearing a red-checked shirt too heavy for late spring, and he was sweating. "You got a lot of junk, you know?"

She smiled her coolest smile. "Am I supposed to apologize?"

"Do what you want." He was deciding whether to get out the same way he got in, his eyes were traveling over the walls, the moldings, the ceiling.

"Take it easy," she said, almost maternally, "I'm not calling the police. I just—I wish you'd wash your hands before you go around fingering everything." She was relieved he wasn't Willie, who would have terrified her.

He nodded gravely, then laughed. "Oh, lady. Clean your fence out there—" He gestured to the back window with his head. The curtains in Wendy's room were gusting out lazily and she could see the inky handprints on the jamb all the way to the front. The cops said they couldn't lift them off that kind of paint; he must know that.

She approached a step. "Well, I wasn't expecting you."

Who did he look like—Yogi Berra? Some baseball player, PeeWee Reese? She had rooted for the Yankees when she was little; California didn't have a single major league team of its own back then. Now she could vaguely see their faces, the swarthy ones with five-o'clock shadow explaining how they had met the ball on the 3-2 pitch. Hank Bauer with her pearls in his pocket.

He sat down on the couch gingerly; suddenly his clothes must have felt very dirty to him, she saw him hunch as though to make himself lighter. She handed him a beer.

"So—you always entertain guys who come in the back window and swipe your stuff?"

She shrugged. "Doesn't happen so often. We probably haven't been here long enough."

"You don't look so mad."

She looked at him with what she knew was an inscrutable face. She felt very good; a funny kind of power it gave you to catch someone right in the middle of a compromising act. Martin did nothing compromising. In all things he did the equivalent of undressing in the closet.

"You look like you have a family, you could have a regular job, if you wanted." His dirty hands made him look as though he was on his way home from work with a lunch box and thermos. Maybe he was. Certainly he didn't have the knife-eyed desperation of an addict.

"Lady—" He spread those hands wide. She was asking him what kind of wine he liked.

She shook her head at herself impatiently. "Well, I suppose you're what we had to have next."

He raised one eyebrow politely. How much should a caught burglar talk? A problem for Amy Vanderbilt.

She looked off. Surviving—the cost of it was going up like the price of milk. She began, patiently. "We moved here from Los Angeles because we were in the earthquake."

In it? Like being in the war? In a play? Yes, in. Among the objects tossed and plummeted. Or within range. Yes, like in the war. The Blitz. Whatever.

"San Fernando, actually. Our house—the back of it, you know—the garage and sun porch and my kitchen, I was in my kitchen—were hanging over a cliff. In about a second—" She snapped her fingers. "My daughter, she's nine? She was playing out back and she came in to get something, a glass of milk, I don't remember, and before she could go back out again there was no back yard."

He was looking at her with steady eyes, keeping quiet.

"Every other thing broke—glass and pictures and a stone vase I had? And things kept tumbling, falling downhill. I close my eyes and everything turns over like—I don't know." She laughed to disparage it. "You know those rides in the amusement park?"

"Yeah, that turn all the way over? You sit on them?"

"It's like that, I get dizzy when I close my eyes so I don't sleep any more. A little, it's getting a little better."

He blinked. "You ought to go to a doctor or something, get some pills, they'll put you out."

"Did you ever go without a lot of sleep?"

He looked up from his beer, considering the question slowly, like a taste. "During the war I did, yeah, in the foxholes. You figured you went to sleep you'd never wake up."

"That's true," she said distantly; she didn't really want to share it, it couldn't have been the same, the suddenness. He probably enlisted, went looking for trouble. She could see him in khakis, his dark hair clipped, his obedient small-dog face snapping to attention, saluting. "That's true. A soldier would . . ."

She had slipped so far, so deep in her dreaming, she

had become part of the landslide forever, she held one
of the timbers of the porch like someone thrown clear
of a wrecked ship and she fell over and over, neat as a
hoop, she must have been curled in a ball, a baby,
knees up, bumping over stones and boulders, into the
center where the earth was hot. Everyone was there,
her neighbors were being stirred, heads bobbed out of
the stew, popped up like bubbles all around, boiling,
then sank back and it closed over. It was all silent,
silence seemed right, it went with the suddenness; faster
than sound, all of it. What was the broth made of?
Molten bones and rock and blood and the earth's own
spring water. Top soil, bottom soil, granite shoulders,
sand and grass. A dog bone flew past and vanished.
Men and women and animals and the roots of trees
were thrown up embracing and fell back in slow motion;
still tangled they made an opening in the soup and
vanished, leaving circles in circles in circles. She
skimmed across the surface—a rock skimming, once,
three times, seven times, good!—feeling her scraped
side, raw, and sank into darkness, and breathed one
time only and her lungs were black, charred, gone.
She had to scream and felt them try to inflate. But they
were full of holes, burst balloons, blood balloons gone
lacy and dark. Each time it ended there, like a movie.
Nothing more till she started it up again. It made her
infinitely weary.

"So my husband said we'd better leave. I was very
upset. Coming apart, kind of." She laughed, pulling
hard on the fingers of one hand with the other, tugging
at herself as though she were a scarf. "You don't have
earthquakes here," she said simply.

He had listened very carefully, his hands in his lap
looking cut loose, nothing to do with them, company
posture. His beer was finished.

"No earthquakes, no tornadoes I don't think. Hurri-
canes once in a while. Snowstorms . . ." It was a tone
he would use on his children, if he had children: full
of tact and the distance of years, of small wisdom out
of which even a two-bit second-story man could fashion small assurances.'

"Robberies," she said, smiling bitterly. "Muggings."
"Rapes."

She would not tell him how she was closed up by it, cauterized. Here and there her skin puckered with memory. She got through the day. She got through the night. Martin asked her one night, turning from her, taking his hand off her shoulder, "Where the hell are you anyway?"

So she played it out, denial, reassurance, careful kisses applied to his neck where he liked them, put in place just so, like a salve. But she was gone off by herself, going nowhere she couldn't keep an eye on everything she owned. And yet she let it go so easily, her rings, her radio . . . The earth wasn't solid. "We could all do with a little less passion," she said once, sharply, just as he was moving into her, and Martin— proud of what he called his "regularity" in bed as though it had something to do with prunes—had gone slack, furiously, and rolled her away roughly like a stone in the garden. It was like being closed tight, sewn by the heat at the center of the earth. Isn't plastic sewn up that way? Then she was plastic, flesh-colored, clean, and everything stayed either outside or inside. Martin had suggested "Getting Help." But she was not guilty and God knows there was nothing to analyze because she was not to blame. Even his damn insurance policies exempted acts of God.

She looked at her caught man coolly. He was shaking his head. Pitying her?

"Don't you believe me?"

"Sure I do. Why not? I saw all that on the news, the six-o'clock news. All them bodies, listen. You're damn lucky."

She sipped her beer. Wendy would be coming home soon. She had to get dinner. "So now you come along."

"Listen, nobody ever said I was a earthquake. You don't watch out I'm gonna be flattered." He laughed, still looking at her strangely, as though from behind something. "I mean, I crowbar your window, I take a couple things out, most of it ain't much good to me anyway—"

"You sell it? Take it to somebody?"

He picked up his empty beer can and looked under it. "You got your friendly neighborhood fence right down there, don't you know Anthony's?" The dark little store where everything lay sunk under years of dust. She had wondered what moved through those bleak aisles, since it clearly wasn't groceries. "Come on, everybody knows Anthony," he said firmly. She bought milk there, expecting it to be sour.

"You shouldn't have told me that."

"Oh lady you couldn't of been here long, like you say. No secret! Tony does a good business, the cops deal down there too so, you know—no sweat."

No, she didn't want to know. Strike it from the record.

Now, how do you get rid of a burglar nicely, she wondered, and felt like a schoolteacher. Something about her dispassionate slightly disapproving face; she felt thinlipped, as though she were someone she'd known once and hadn't especially liked. That and her indifference at the core: Only till three, then I go home. She was very tired; breathing was hard under this damn dirty sky.

So she stood, feeling strong in her indifference. "Well, what do I do with you now? What you took was worth a lot."

"You don't look too stung."

She felt scolded. "That doesn't matter. That stuff is expensive to replace." He had probably looked in their bankbook.

He smiled. "So don't replace it."

"Is that what we have to expect from now on? Strangers walking through our house putting their dirty hands on everything?"

"Jesus, that dirt really gets you, don't it? You ought to meet my mother, you'd get along."

She stood up and paced like some woman on a soap opera, distraught on a small stage. "God, every place I turn. I feel like the apocalypse is coming, bit by bit dribbling away . . ."

"Take it easy, I ain't no earthquake. I ain't a member of the acopalypse. I live in Red Hook, I'm a little hard up, O.K.? I don't even do this regular, so relax."

She gave him a sour look. "Why don't you just go? Only give me what you've taken today. I want that back."

He looked at her, head to foot, as he stood up. "Thanks for the beer," he said quietly in an ordinary voice, a bank teller asking if she'd take singles. "Hey, try to relax a little. You'll make it better. There ain't gonna be no earthquake, you better believe it. Mayor don't allow it." He turned and walked to the front door, unhurried, leaving the footprints of his heavy work shoes on the rug. The cops couldn't get those either. He turned both locks casually, without the usual scrutiny that distracted her visitors from their good-bys. "I'll wash my hands next time." He closed the door exactly as Martin did, sturdily, with one quick push from outside to make sure the lock had clicked.

She sat down on the couch where he'd been sitting. It was so warm it was almost damp. Evisceration, she said to herself, turning the word over, thinking of chickens. Some women get their insides plucked out at around her age anyway. Same difference only cheaper, no Blue Cross. Her womb, her guts, all that dark eternally dangerous stuff stolen. Before it explodes. Dried up; out of business; kaput. Even if Willie came in that window with its curtains dancing up and out, and wanted what was left of her, right here and now before dinner, he'd jimmy her open and find her gone. The only way to make it in New York, she said to herself, and stood up wearily to get the chops out of the freezer. Spread the word.

❧

253

❧

CECIL AND AMELIA

It wasn't beautiful but he loved his life. Just for now it was being something more important than beautiful, it was adding up, making little black tracks like ant rows under his name at that bank downtown that looked like a national monument. When the time came he would cash it all in and buy back some of that beauty he knew was there and live in it forever, half-asleep. It was a reasonable plan. He felt clean and honest and lucky.

Maybe that was the thing that set him apart: having found little peacefulness here—Brooklyn, Harlem, anywhere—still he knew where there were incredible dark caves and piles of sweet turbot lying beached under a sky that never blinked. And he trusted it to stay there: in the Islands, the village where he had been dust-poor and barefooted, but where the sunlight and the blues and reds and flaring yellows burned all around him, real. He remembered his life, in childhood, as a place without roofs, without walls. He was wrong, of course—his own house and the bar his father worked in, swept out mornings, where he rolled garbage cans in and out of the back, humming—they were moist and dark all day, and buggy, rank with fruit rinds souring in the heat. But a man has got control, Cecil would think; he can remember what he wants to, like, say it was the best place on some woman's body instead of all of her, say not the warts on her chin or her barrel ass. What if you like one spot, a softish place that you get to know—then she's good enough, yes? Good enough. So: there was a cove, it was a good forty miles from his falling-down village, but he dreamed of the one time he'd got there on Uncle Cat's truck, on the way to somewhere: water the color of nothing he'd

27

ever seen—the closest thing to it was a screeching
turquoise plastic like Howard Johnson's but that sure
as hell didn't look like water. Soft mountains of sand
that seemed to breathe; warmth all the time, pillowy,
without edges.

For this dream Cecil got up, though none too early,
and went forth with his big gray exterminator's box,
like a tool kit, a doctor's bag. "Oh no, don't laugh,"
he told people, smiling, his very dark pocky cheeks
full as a squirrel's, his squirrelly teeth showing their
points. "If you have a fat mouse or a rat in your baby's
crib, I'm better than the family doctor, don't you tell
me no. And here"—laying down pink powder in
generous rows the opposite of seed, killer seed—"here's
your prescription. He pick this up on his little dumb
feet and then stop to lick off his toes and—" Snaps
his fingers, shakes his head, pops his eyes as though
he is witnessing a bombing. His face is at its best when
it is comic.

He thought of his father sometimes, old now but still
working, whenever he hummed, pushing aside a refrigerator or laying a noxious trail of cunning pink mayhem
along the baseboard behind a heavy sofa. Papa would
sing, "Oh lady, la-dy of mornings, la-day of moon-
folly nights" in a complicated mongrel calypso beat.
Soon, soon, he would answer himself, I have me a
lady for moon-folly and go down the cove and sleep
for ninety-nine years in the sun. Soon. He'd be with
his old mama, his teetering papa before it was too late,
and his beautiful little sisters whom he loved, who had
always run faster than he did and were thin as coconut
fronds.

Meanwhile, with the money from his work, he was
collecting apartment houses. Well, no, he'd stopped
calling them that because a girl he'd met at a dance
had seen one and said, "Mon, you liar! That no apartment, that a dinky little doghouse, hey!" They were
rental properties or renovation sites now; duplexes,
triplexes soon. The times were right; when he could
get more capital, after the investments, he would fix
them up with pine board and lots of kitchens and rent
them at a good price, no joke. People on this block
were charging three hundred dollars for *half* a doghouse,

with shutters and a gate to keep the junkies back. He didn't like people who kid themselves and get laughed at, but he was going to get out with his money and go home. This was such a reasonable plan he could even get a loan if he needed one.

So he lived in the house at 253 and the other ones, a few miles deeper into Brooklyn on a less showy block that hung, undecided, just outside the ghetto, he kept well shoveled in winter, neatly swept in summer. They had a couple of shoddy flower boxes which were vandalized regularly, flowers ripped in handfuls and flung down on the steps or stomped into the cement like cigarette butts. He was still amazed to be a landlord, with a shy kind of power his money had bought. He was utterly benevolent with his tenants, to the point where benevolence didn't even enter in. He hated to be made self-conscious for being fair. They were his friends living there, or the family of emigrating friends, and they kept him feeling close to home. Their rooms were small and dark and the chipped paint was a kind of welfare-office-green, but they were cheap and warm and there weren't any mice or silverfish, he could promise them that! Huge ailanthus trees leaned outside the rear windows, with long loose leaves that reminded him of what he'd grown up with; he enjoyed telling people they were only weeds, as wild as they looked. Even in Brooklyn, weeds lodged in the cracks and grew lush as tropical bushes. They were much more comforting than those puny little thoroughbreds the block association had planted in front of every other house, mangy and bony, promising a spot of shade in twenty years. Oh no! They weren't for him.

The house was full of the lovely start-stop rhythm of West Indian voices and from time to time he gave a party in the dank little yard which he had cemented over (despairing of real grass) and painted with a big colorful star. Everyone brought beer and they had lobster and crabs and barbecue, and they sang, the girls always in colors that moved in and out slowly like flags in wind. If the neighbors complained of the noise he would invite them along too, and mean it, black or white, though the complainers were the least likely to come.

He would pick a girl who looked particularly luscious

that night, one who made him miss home where the
girls wore less clothing and gave in without much fuss,
and he would have her stay the night in his indifferently
furnished room. Once in a while a girl wouldn't stay
but usually—he smiled a lot, his whole face, forehead,
cheeks, chin breaking into many horizontal lines and
gullies—he made them unself-conscious enough to think
they'd have a good time, lots of contented beer-warmed
laughing and a straightforward not unkind few minutes
of loving in his big rumpled bed under a green chenille
spread. Cecil was a self-absorbed lover, who rode from
minute to minute without much sense of what could
be—whatever was, was, and they both went to meet
it. And he never looked back, nor felt himself suddenly
beached, abandoned, empty. He had a smile for after-
wards that made a girl feel she'd done something very
innocent and sisterly. The very few girls who started
out in his bed learned very little from him, but they
never cried.

Cecil had one brother in Philadelphia, with whom
he had occasional lusty reunions, and another, the
youngest, had promised to come if he would send the
fare. But instead he got a letter from his parents. Henry
had a job and wasn't leaving until he got sacked. But
his little sister, Amelia, wanted to come instead. He
had made it sound like a friendly place, she liked to
work hard and would get a job. They wrote: "She is
no kind of a city girl, big-city woman or move fast,
but she try if you help her some." He screwed his face
into a prune thinking, straining to remember. Amelia
and Sissie tended to get mixed up in his memories.
They were skinny as clothes hangers and slept in one
bed, shared their few clothes between them, laughed
most of the time, provoking everyone and everything
to laugh with them. They even taught the dog to make
a weird noise they swore was real laughing. He and
the other boys had spent a lot of time running past
them, pulling at the tops of their dresses, when they
were about eleven or twelve, maybe, trying to get a
peek at those little raisins they kept inside. It was Sissie
who had a boyfriend, though, and then a child and had
gone to St. Croix with her man last year. So Amelia
was probably lonely. He sent her money for a one-way

plane ticket with enough left over to get a pretty dress.
"Get a red dress, you look nice in red," he told her,
half-lying, half-remembering—well, she was pretty
dark, and had to look good in it. He hoped it would
have tiny sprigs of may-flowers on it, or forget-me-nots
with their yellow eyes. Little sisters were very blessed
buds.

So Amelia came. From a distance, as she waved to
him from the other side of the customs counter, he
thought there had been a mistake, that she had sent a
friend who remembered or had been briefed about how
to know him. But it was Amelia's little voice that
seemed to come from some small part of her, one toe,
maybe, and a certain cock of the head was hers, though
he found it more skeptical than he remembered it, less
teasing. When she embraced him he was astonished at
how much bosom—stony and seasoned, it felt—came
between them. Godalmighty, had he been away all that
long? Really? He tried to make a joke—"Ah, you caught
up with our mama there, hanh, you passed her right
by!" But she looked at him without smiling. Well,
what was it about her? She was thick, this girl. Solid
and unhumorous, with a flat face that made him think,
apologetically, of the robots he sometimes saw in the
movies, made of tin. She was wearing the dress she
had bought for the trip—she thanked him for it dutifully. It was navy blue, with a wide stiff belt that seemed
to be part of her figure; that secured her and was not
graceful.

They ran through the news of home before their exit
on the Belt Parkway, because she gave no details. Uncle
Cat's funeral? Well, it was terrible, like a melee. Papa's
health kept him from working regularly, his back was
getting arthritic. Sissie she would not talk about, not a
word. She was sitting straight beside him, her face
forward, only her eyes taking in the long ranges of
buildings, Sixty-fourth Street, Twenty-eighth Street, the
angles of the stoops and the spidery fire escapes repeated
and repeated like furrows, planted fields, where nothing changed but the color of the brick and the promises
on those billboards up over the roofs, banks that gave
a million per cent on your money and beer that massaged

the back of your head, cars that drove you straight to
kingdom come. The traffic coiled and uncoiled, the big
red sign that said BATTERY TUNNEL TRAFFIC KEEP
LEFT came on them out of the dusk suddenly and he
had to change lanes fast, making his way between two
bumpers already pocked with dents.

"Are you wild?" his sister asked him quietly, still
looking straight ahead.

"Am I wild? What you mean, wild? Everything
depends." He was smiling at the possibilities.

She had no answer but she looked disapproving. Her
face was so flat, she had swept everything off it—
what, with the back of her hand?—and out of the
corners of her eyes and down, unimpeded, rolled two
incredibly large tears. Oh, sentimental, he thought.
Girls must get scared away from home, Mama so far
away her face was getting invisible.

"Don't be scared," he said gently. "You got nothin'
to be scared about." He reached out for her knee but
nothing was there.

She turned her head a little to look at him and he
thought he could see himself, a little black dot, reflected
in her nearest globe of a tear, before it fell off her
cheek.

He had installed her in the little room at the top of
the stairs, sparsely furnished like everything else in the
house but clean—Cecil had brought a respect for the
all-week washday from home—and its barred windows
looked out into the real-green shade of those fake weed
trees. "You put your dresses here—and look yourself
over here, all round the crack if you can do it—and
sleep here, two pillows. You bring anybody home, hon,
nobody in this house going to ask no questions." She
gave him that look again, and he wondered for a fleeting second if she liked men. She acted like the nuns
he'd known, whom he and his friends had considered
raping, just to see if they had what they needed, or
were defective to begin with.

He showed her around downtown Brooklyn, where
she regarded the high slick façades of the department
stores in that same stern silence. If she felt any of those
stirrings at the mannequins in the windows which he

(having walked here with one pretty girl or another)
thought automatic in her sex, she gave no hint. Even
he liked to look at them; half these days were painted
chocolate brown with saucy eyes and wigs made of
steel wool, the others blond and bony and more bare
each year.

She did say she was going out one morning to see
about a salesgirl's job on Fulton Street but nothing
apparently came of it. He was sitting on the front steps
with Hector, his oldest tenant, who drove a cab and
came home at odd hours, like he did. They were finish-
ing a beer when Amelia came down the street, fast.
She walked forward on her feet a little in big broken-in
shoes. Heavy as she was, she always seemed to be
fleeing.

He raised his whole forehead, not just his eyebrows,
to ask how it went. She murmured and edged past him.
So he asked her right out. She didn't answer till she
was halfway up the dark stairs. Then she shouted back,
on a note so angry it sounded like the climax of a long
loud argument. "Your Americans, they stink!"

"My Americans!" Cecil said, and, laughing,
collapsed his beer can.

It was a good season, very hot and buggy. Cecil was
working every day, home most nights, but he rarely saw
Amelia. She didn't eat with him. Sometimes he forgot she
was there, in that closet of a room all day with her door
closed, not even a radio. Or he would knock on her door
and she would be standing there, neatly dressed at any
hour, mute as a brick. "I thought you must be hatching
two dozen eggs," he would say lightly, or something like
it, not wanting to seem too distressed. Her smooth brown
face was a field lying fallow.

"Maybe you ought to charge her some rent," one of
his roomers suggested pointedly. "Then she'd have to
get out and work."

But he was her brother and he couldn't do that.

With summer on, he invited her to dances, to parties,
in vain. His own parties raged cheerfully under her
window but he never so much as caught her peeking
down on them.

He sent girls to her when they seemed the right

combination of gentleness and strength. She would not talk. One, a sweet young nurse's aide (up early to find Cecil already above her and working hard), was already dressed, one Monday morning, in her white stockings and her heavy-soled shoes. She tapped on Amelia's door and asked her if she thought she might like to come see about a job at the hospital.

"Well, Cecil—dear?—she isn't so much taller than me but she looked down on me the whole time. I don't know how but I could feel it, you know?—just glaring down on the top of my head! Her eyes aren't anything like yours . . ." She stood in his loose embrace as if for comfort. "Honey, I hate to say it but I think there's something a little the matter with her." She sounded as though she was prodding an injured animal with her toe. Cecil thanked her for trying, a little embarrassed, and walked her to the door feeling especially defiant, his hands on her hips from behind.

What happened with Hector—well, if it had been the only thing he might have sympathized with her. His old friend was a champion class skirt-chaser. (These days it was pants.) He was young, looked younger, and made the most of his premeditated innocence. Even the spaces between his teeth made girls want to protect him, somehow they thought they could barricade him against the world with their bodies. Cecil found him a good laugh, the way he went after any shadow that passed, like a baby duck looking for his mama.

He knew all that but it didn't make Hector intimidating. One morning he went to the kitchen, absently—his mind was on the tax assessor who was meeting him at his other houses—and found Amelia standing flattened against the refrigerator. Her eyes had the look of a screaming woman though her mouth was shut tight, and she was holding the can opener in her hand. It was the jagged kind with points above and below, like a crawfish, that made Cecil nervous. She held it tightly but not carefully.

Hector was sitting in a chair, his arm across the back casually. He had a smile but it wasn't working.

Cecil waited.

Finally Hector said impatiently (because she wasn't

pretty), "Look, mon, call her off, can you? I didn't do nothing here, didn't think a thought even, not today. I'm eating a grapefruit right now, reading the box score."

Cecil reached for the can opener as though he expected her to give it to him, and she did. "So what the problem?"

His sister looked choked on adrenalin, he could see her heart, one whole breast, quaking behind the dark robe she wore buttoned to the throat. "His eyes too nervy for his own good," she said fiercely. "I call them, they put you in jail."

Hector folded his *Daily News* elaborately; she hugged her robe so tight she had to hobble past them to the stairs.

"You know I never was no morning mon, Cecil," he finally said. "Even if she had the stuff, mon, sun ain't even out of bed yet, what she want from me?"

This kind of thing only made Cecil impatient. He knew there were women who dreamed themselves into corners, hoped themselves, and then screamed murder and pulled switchblades, yah, yah. If she had to see what wasn't there why couldn't she find something better than Hector's bloodshot eyes. Uncle Cat's first wife saw visions of Lucifer—anyway she called him Lucifer in her naggy voice, just the way she pecked at Cat. After every baby she had, she got a visit from him, then he must have had enough and went home. And a kid in his village, an albino kid who never went to school even for a single day, Cecil remembered he used to walk up to people and tell them he had copperheads in a basket he carried around his neck and unless they gave him a coin or something bright-colored, when he let them free everyone would fall over dead. That kind of dreaming-up Cecil could see, it came from some mysterious pit he wouldn't think of approaching. But this stuff, this no-touch-me business, was that all her silence was made of? He spat into the sink and went downstairs as noisily as he could manage.

Cecil had a dream. In it he was sitting up on the beach tying tags around the legs of pigeons, eating endless fish whose bones towered beside him, intricately woven, a cage of them, and what should the rising tide wash

in but a woman. She was naked but her body was
blank, as if the details of her flesh had been washed
away. Then he saw her eyes were open, but they were
washed blank too. Like a marble statue she floated up
among the pigeons who poked at her with their vague
curious concentration. The dream didn't frighten him,
it had that same helpless blighted feeling Amelia inspired
in him awake. As though a blow to the head had blunted
her senses, or a late frost. He believed dreams, they
told truths he always recognized, and this one seemed
not so much a promise as a description of what already
was. He was not frightened, only sad.

The next afternoon he got home feeling determined.
He marched into the house like an angry father. The
front room was too dark to see in but it felt empty.
Nothing breathed there but his fish in their lurid green
tank. They poured around corners, drained of sound;
if they were his watchmen they were mute. He walked
up the bare stairs as quietly as he could, though he
hadn't really wanted to be sneaking up on her. Doors
were closed, there was no music. He hadn't realized
how sour the dust smelled up here. He knocked softly
on Amelia's paint-chipped closet door. No rustle, no
breath. He knocked louder, finally turned the knob
slowly, feeling the tension against his slippery palm.

Amelia was asleep on the bed, face down, wearing
a khaki raincoat he hadn't ever seen on her. She slept
like a beached whale—large, slowly breathing, complete.
One bare buttock half-showed, where the rumpled coat
was hiked up under her. He stood above her and looked
down at the shadowy globe of his sister's flesh. In
some strange but very distinct way far from words he
felt he would be presuming more if he tried to see her
face, where it was sunk like a secret in the folds of her
pillows. What did he know about her but the two things
that made her his sister—her name and the way her
girlhood had looked to him as he ran by? Not to her, to
him; her girlhood, not her womanhood. She had made
herself ugly, almost, as no one in his family was ugly:
they were transparent, clear-water, all of them, so wiry
and small, and here her little ass—it had been that, at
sixteen, you knew you could hold it in one hand like a
baby's if you could catch her long enough—now her

little ass was this smooth and massive stone that turned away the light. And touching? Some round women had to be touched. He had loved one once for a year, had lived lost in her, like a big stuffed rust-colored armchair. But he could not imagine fingers on this cold rump or those gourd breasts she tried to hide behind clumpy cotton. If he pressed his thumbs into her—he had to put his hands behind his back—surely she would give no more than a stone. He wished he could turn her over and look to see: was she a virgin? Is that what the business with Hector was all about? Did she bear terrible scars, like some women he'd seen, betrayed by crazy lovers? Did she have long stripes of marbled skin stretched loose by a bastardy baby? Was she carrying one this minute under all that dull thick clothing?

He left her room that was heavy with breathed air, and went to get a beer to quell a quivering like anger that stirred his stomach.

No matter the excuse he invented to go and talk to Amelia, she gave the same answer: round eyes that glistened with the threat of heavy unshed tears. She seemed to be telling him he should understand, that the special privilege of a brother should be to leave her alone as no one else would. He wrote home urgently: What happened to my sister? What's this you sent me? Did you send her away to go crazy or what? Listen, this is a no-good idea, a stranger! I can't help her. There was no reply. Answers took time but he knew he would get none. Were his parents afraid to answer him?

Finally, tired of futile gentleness—she looked at him as though he were abusing her but said not one word in self-defense—he tried to shake her. It was only a corner of his anger but he thought, had to think, it might have worked. It was a calculated risk, based on his certainty of what he'd have done if anyone had spoken to him that way. So he had shouted at her that she was acting like a cow, that she was lazy and too fat and unwashed, that he couldn't stand her dumb tears. "Tell me what they supposed to be for, hanh? What kind of secrets eating you up alive? I never knew nothing that matters this much. Nothing. No one." He had shocked himself, his vehemence, his philosophiz-

ing. Who was this man who had a strange sister here
and a foolish brother protesting there, and couldn't do
anything that had to be done? He was floating far from
himself; he hated to come home from his days of killing off mice and sealing the doors that cockroaches
made for themselves—there at least he knew what he
was doing, and he could see what a difference it made.
People thanked him.

Then abruptly it was finished. It was a Friday. He
had come around the corner as far as the top end of a
traffic jam, but it was too early in the afternoon for
that. There were police cars down at his end of the
block. Hector? Had she got him arrested for sure this
time? He was stuck in his car. Finally he just got out
and left it there, nobody was going anywhere anyway,
in spite of all the honking and cursing. He sprinted
down the street. The thick knot he'd been carrying in
his stomach was coming undone already, letting go, no
matter what. It was over, something was, and what had
been stuck had come dislodged without his knowing
it, while he was riding down Flatbush Avenue listening
to the Mets. Every hard slap of his foot to the uneven
sidewalk knocked him closer to a feeling of relief.

The sidewalk in front of his house was a vast puddle
of broken glass. Howard Peet from 255 was standing
on his steps like the official greeter.

"What is all this?" Cecil asked him. There was a
crowd that held itself back like an audience.

"Listen, Fontaine, somebody from your house has
been throwing bottles down."

"Throwing bottles! When?"

Peet thought, checked his watch, which looked like
it could launch a space ship, and said, "Maybe around
two they started. Hit the bus, right on the bumper,
shattered the damn thing all around. Threw one at the
Pacheco kid and got her smack on the ear." He shook
his head angrily. "Had to take her to get stitches."

Cecil emptied his face. He felt a hostile cold in his
stomach, just under his belt. He was heading up the
steps. "Did you see anybody?"

Peet had a face that came to a point, everything
perfectly aimed for snooping; a face like the tail of a
dog.

"Hm-mh. Just an arm. I think there's some in the back too. I heard the glass breaking."

He took the rest of the steps in one bound.

They have shouldered in the door on the upstairs stoop. There is a long angry crack the whole way down and it's been flung back so hard it's swung half shut again. Will they drag her down, she covering her face like some criminal or kicking at their navy shins? The kids from Caspian Street who are always hitting each other are standing still for once, craning their necks there's such a crowd to see around. Somebody yells "When they gonna come *out?*" just as Cecil meets them coming down the pitch-dark hall. They are walking gently, bringing her along, but not the way they drag someone they're arresting. They are making their way step by step looking straight ahead, grim as tango dancers. It bursts in front of his eyes in the total night of his rooming-house hall—anything at all, a melted candle in a bowl, Amelia dissolved to wax, like something in a fairy tale, bewitched. Curdled to soured milk, that rancid smell coming closer. Blood wrung from a towel. Amelia?

He flattens himself against the wall, arms out like a prisoner himself. They murmur something he doesn't catch, something intended as condolence, or an order to follow them, or an obscenity, and pass him like piano movers carrying gingerly between their four massive navy and gold shoulders the raincoat crumpled but no flesh showing. No face. Her barren face broken under there. If she doesn't need the air to breathe, would they be dragging her out, they'd have photographers, they'd be putting up ropes, they'd have an ambulance even so. No? No? There is a maddening silence outside—they're getting what they were waiting for or maybe it's not bloody enough—and Cecil, standing on the runner that's been harrowed by years of his friends' feet, is trying to shout down the vehement disgust he feels.

Mama Harriette, Papa Cyrus, they sent him this message in a broken bottle. Goddamn them. "I don't want no goddamn mysteries in my goddamn house!" he hisses to the bony ribs of the radiator, shaking it. "Who in the hell come in here, call herself my sister, just like that?"

There are black blotches on the rug, they have splashed into the fibers, spreading everywhere, her pain. Someone comes thumping up the stone steps, not Peet, a strange white kid, and shouts, "Hey man, they're waiting and you better go move your car, you got all Brooklyn honking all the way to Smith Street."

He starts. "Don't get excited, mon, I come in my good time." He looks back up the stairs at the end of the hall, as though she might still be up there. He would beat that stony ass of hers if he had it to beat, that bitch filled up with self-pity like a jug of wine to rot your eyes out, that stinking hole that he couldn't see to the bottom of. What she come here to do to him, hex him till he shout O.K.? *O.K. what?*

He slams the door but its hinges are torn and it hits the jamb with a muffled thud and leaps wide open. Leaving the whole house open, asking for trouble. He'll thank the cops if anything's missing when he gets back. The late afternoon is cold against his sweaty sides. When he was a kid he used to feel that quick rebuking chill so often, every day, one thing or another, after he peed down his leg or walked through a new puddle or ran along the ocean picking up conch for supper. He'd be punished, he'd get a cuffing but Papa would mutter, "Boys, boys, never was a boy, be live or dead, didn't dry up in the sun *some* time." What did she do to him dripping all over his rug, withering fast? . . . Papa smiled so long without teeth, like a wince. And knew what happened today. Everyone but him knew, him, Cecil, letting out the hand brake of his car so the traffic could move, pulling it in front of the hydrant because there'd be no parking for a mile around, right into a lake of broken shimmering, like rock salt, seeing just the top of his wide forehead in the mirror where he slouched, pulling up straight against that perplexed unpitying stare in the eyes that says, "Cecil? Fontaine, that one? He gone away, don't know where. Give him a couple of days, you come back, look again. Only a goddamn fool know more than that." Pocketing his key, he gets into the back of the patrol car angry, with the face of an accuser.

❦

255

❦

HOW TO WIN

All they need at school is permission on a little green card that says *Keep this child at bay. Muffle him, tie his hands, his arms to his ankles, anything at all. Distance, distance. Dose him.* And they gave themselves permission. They never even mentioned a doctor, and their own certified bureaucrat in tweed (does he keep a badge in his pocket like the cops?) drops by the school twice a year for half a day. But I insisted on a doctor. And did and did, had to, because Howard keeps repeating, vaguely, that he is "within the normal range of boyish activity."

"But I live with it, all day every day."

"It? Live with *it?*"

Well, Howard can be as holy as he likes, I am his mother and I will not say "him." Him is the part I know, Christopher, my first child and first son, the boy who was a helpless warm mound once in a blue nightie tied at the bottom to keep his toes in. ("God, Margaret, you are dramatic and sentimental and sloppy. How about being realistic for a change?") "It" is what races around my room at night, a bat, pulling down the curtain cornice, knocking over the lamps, tearing the petals off the flowers.

Watch Christopher take a room sometime; that's the word for it, like an army subduing a deserted plain. He stands in the doorway always for one extra split-split second, straining his shoulders down as though he's hitching himself to some machine, getting into harness. He has no hips, and round little six-year-old shoulders that look frail but are made of welded steel that has no give when you grab them. Then what does he see ahead of him? I'm no good at guessing. The room is an

43

animal asleep, trusting the air, its last mistake. (See, I am sympathetic to the animal.) He leaps on it and leaves it disemboweled, then turns his dark eyes to me where I stand—when I stand; usually I'm dervishing around trying to stop the bloodshed—and they ask me Where did it go? What happened? Who killed this thing, it was just breathing, I wanted to *play* with it. Christopher. When you're not here to look at me I have to laugh at your absurd powers. You are incontinent, you leak energy. As for me, I gave birth to someone else's child.

There is a brochure inside the brown bottle that the doctor assigned us, very gay, full-color, busy with children riding their bicycles right through patches of daffodils, sleeping square in the middle of their pillows, doing their homework with a hazy expression to be attributed to concentration, not medication. NONADDICTIVE! NO SIGNIFICANT SIDE EFFECTS! Dosage should decrease by or around puberty. Counterindications epilepsy, heart and circulatory complications, severe myopia and related eye problems. See *Journal of Pediatric Medicine*, III 136, F '71; *Pharmacology Bulletin*, v. 798, 18, pp. 19–26, D '72. CAUTION: DO NOT ALLOW CHILDREN ACCESS TO PILLS! SPECIAL FEATURE: U-LOK-IT CAP! REMEMBER, TEACH YOUR CHILD THE ETIQUETTE OF THE MEDICINE CABINET.

I know how he dreams me. I know because I dream his dreams. He runs to hide in me. Battered by the stick of the old dark he comes fast, hiccoughing terror. By the time I am up, holding him, it has hobbled off, it must be, into his memory. I've pulled on a robe, I spread my arms—do they look winged or webbed?— to pull him out of himself, hide him, swear the witch is nowhere near. He doesn't go to his father. But he won't look at my face.

It was you! He looks up at me finally and says nothing but I see him thinking. So: *I* was the witch, with a club behind my bent back. I the hundred-stalked flower with webbed branches. I with the flayed face held in my two hands like a bloody towel. Then how can I help him?

I whisper to him, wordless; just a music. He answers, "Mama." It is a faint knocking, through layers of dirt, through flowers.

His sister Jody will dream those dreams, and all the children who will follow her. I suppose she will, like chicken pox every child can expect them: there's a three o'clock in the dark night of children's souls too, let's not be too arrogant taking our prerogatives. But if she does, she'll dream them alone, no accomplices. I won't meet her halfway, give her my own last fillip, myself in shreds.

I've been keeping a sort of log: a day in the life. For no purpose, since my sense of futility runs deeper than any data can testify to. Still it cools me off.

He is playing with Jacqueline. They are in the Rosenbergs' yard. C. is on his way to the sandbox which belongs to Jackie's baby brother, Seth, so I see trouble ahead. I will not interfere. No, *intervene* is the word they use. Interfere is not as objective, it's the mess that parents make, as opposed to the one the doctors make. As he goes down the long narrow yard at a good clip C. pulls up two peonies, knocks over Seth's big blond blocky wooden horse (for which he has to stop and plant his feet very deliberately, it's that well balanced, i.e., expensive). Kicks over short picket fence around tulips, finally gets to sandbox, walks up to Jackie, whose back is to him, and pushes her hard. She falls against fence and goes crying to her mother with a splinter. She doesn't even bother to retaliate, knowing him too well? Then he leans down into the sand. Turns to me again, that innocent face. It is not conniving, or falsely naïve, I swear it's not. He isn't that kind of clever. Nor is he a gruff bully boy who likes to fly from trees and conquer turf: he has a small peaked face, a little French, I think, in need of one of those common Gallic caps with the beak on the front; a narrow forehead on which his dark hair lies flat like a salon haircut. Anything but a bully, this helpless child of mine—he has a weird natural elegance that terrifies me, as though it is true, what I feel, that he was intended to be someone else. Now he seems to be saying, Well, take all this stuff away if you don't want me to touch

it. Get me out of this goddamn museum. Who says
I'm not provoked? *That's what you say to each other.*

Why is *he* not glass? He will break us all without so
much as chipping.

The worst thing I can think. I am dozing in the sun,
Christopher is in kindergarten, Jody is napping, and I
am guiltily trying to coax a little color into my late-fall
pallor. It's a depressing bleary sun up there. But I sleep
a little, waking in fits and snatches when Migdalia
down the block lets her kid have it and his whine sails
across the yards, and when the bus shakes the earth all
the way under the gas mains and water pipes to China.
The worst thing is crawling through my head like a
stream of red ants: What if he and I, Howie and I, had
been somewhere else way back that night we smiled
and nodded and made Christopher? If the night had
been bone-cracking cold? If we were courting some
aloneness, back to back? But it was summer, we were
married three months, and the bottom sheet was spread
like a picnic cloth. If there is an astrologer's clock,
that's what we heard announcing to us the time was
propitious; but I rehearse the time again. We lived off
Riverside Drive that year and the next, I will float a
thundercloud across the river from the Palisades and
just as Howie turns to me I will have the most extraordinary burst of rain, sludgy and cold, explode through
the open windows everywhere and finish us for the
evening. The rugs are soaked, our books on the desk
are corrugated with dampness, we snap at each other,
Howie breaks a beer glass and blames me. We unmake
him. . . . Another night we will make a different child.
Don't the genes shift daily in their milky medium like
lottery tickets in their fishbowl? I unmake Christopher's skin and bone: egg in the water, blind; a single
sperm thrusts out of its soft side, retreating. Arrow
swimming backwards, tail drags the heavy head away
from life. All the probability in the universe cheers. He
is unjoined. I wake in a clammy sweat. The sun, such
as it was, is caught behind the smokestacks at the far
end of Caspian Street. I feel dirty, as though I've sinned
in my sleep, and there's that fine perpetual silt on my
arms and legs and face, the Con Ed sunburn. I go in

and start making lunch for Christopher, who will survive me.

Log: He is sitting at the kitchen table trying to string kidney beans on a needle and thread. They do it in kindergarten. I forgot to ask why. Jody wakes upstairs, way at the back of the house with her door closed, and C. says quietly, without looking up from his string, "Ma, she's up." It's like hearing something happening, I don't know, a mile away. He has the instincts of an Indian guide, except when I stand right next to him to talk. Then it blows right by.

And when she's up. He seems to make a very special effort to be gentle with his little sister. I can see him forcibly subdue himself, tuck his hands inside his pockets or push them into the loops of his pants so that he loses no honor in restraint. But every now and then it gets the better of him. He walked by her just a minute ago and did just what he does to anything that's not nailed down or bigger than he is: gave her a casual but precise push. The way the bath mat slips into the tub without protest, the glass bowl gets smashed, its pieces settling with a resigned tinkle. I am, of course, the one who's resigned: I hear them ring against each other before they hit the ground, in the silence that envelops the shove.

This time Jody chose to lie back on the rug—fortunately it wasn't cement, I am grateful for small favors—and watch him. An amazing, endearing thing for a two-year-old. I think she has all the control that was meant for the two of them, and this is fair to neither. Eyes wide open, untearful, Jody the antidote, was thinking something about her brother. She cannot say what.

When his dosage has been up a while he begins to cringe before her. It is unpredictable and unimaginable but true and I bear witness to it here. As I was writing the above he ran in and hid behind my chair. Along came J., who had just righted herself after the attack on her; she was pulling her corn popper, vaguely humming. For C., an imagined assault? Provoked? Real? Wished-for?

• • •

Howard, on his way out of the breakfast chaos, bears
his briefcase like a shield, holds it in front of him for
lack of space while he winds his way around the table
in our little alcove, planting firm kisses on our fore-
heads. On his way out the door he can be expected to
say something cheerful and blind to encourage me
through the next unpredictable half hour before I walk
Christopher up the block to school. This morning,
unlocking the front gate I caught him pondering. "Well,
what are other kids like? I mean we've never had any
others so how do we know where they fall on the
spectrum?"

"We know," I said. "What about Jody?"

"Oh," he said, waving her away like a fly. "I mean
boys."

"We also know because we're not knots on logs,
some of us, that's how we know. What was it he did
to your shaver this morning?"

Smashed it to smithereens is what he did, and left
cobweb cracks in the mirror he threw it at.

To which his father shrugged and turned to pull the
gate shut fast.

Why did we have Jody. People dare to ask, astonished, though it's none of their business. They mean,
and expect us to forgive them, how could we take such
a martyr's chance. I tell them that when C. was born I
was ready for a large family. You can't be a secretary
forever, no matter how many smash titles your boss
edits. Nor an administrative assistant, nor an indispensible right hand. I've got my own arms, for which I
need all the hands I've got. I like to be boss, thank
you, in my own house.

But I'll tell you. For a long time I guarded very
tensely against having another baby. C. was hurting
me too much, already he was. Howard would rap with
his fist on my nightgowned side, demanding admission. For a while I played virgin. I mean, I didn't try,
I wasn't playing. He just couldn't make any headway.
I've heard it called dys-something; also crossbones, to
get right down to what it's like. (Dys-something puts
me right in there with my son, doesn't it? I'll bet
there's some drug, some muscle relaxant that bones

you and just lays you out on the knife like a chicken to be stuffed and trussed. . . .) Even though it wasn't his fault I'll never forgive Howard for using his fists on me, even as gently and facetiously as he did. Finally I guess he got tired of trying to disarm me one night at a time, of bringing wine to bed or dancing with me obscenely like a kid at a petting party or otherwise trying to distract me while he stole up on me. So that's when he convinced me to have another baby. I guess it seemed easier. "We'll make Christopher our one exceptional child while we surround him with ordinary ones. We'll grow a goddam garden around him, he'll be outnumbered."

Well—I bought it. We could make this child matter less. It was an old and extravagant solution. Black flowers in his brain, what blight would the next one have, I insisted he *promise* me. He lied, ah, he lied with his hand between my legs, he swore the next would be just as beautiful but timid—"Downright phlegmatic, how's that?"—and would teach Christopher to be human. So I sighed, desperate to believe, and unlocked my thighs, gone rusty and stiff. But I'll tell you, right as he turned out, by luck, to be, I think I never trusted him again, one of my two deceitful boys, because whatever abandon I once had is gone, sure as my waist is gone. I feel it now and Howard is punished for it. Starting right then, making Jody, I have dealt myself out in careful proportions, like an unreliable cook bent only on her batter.

Meanwhile I lose one lamp, half the ivory on the piano keys, and all my sewing patterns to my son in a single day. On the same day I lose my temper, lose it so irretrievably that I am tempted to pop one of Christopher's little red pills myself and go quietly. Who's the most frightening, the skimpy six-year-old flying around on the tail of his bird of prey, or his indispensible right-hand mama smashing the canned goods into the closet with a sound generally reserved for the shooting range? All the worse, off his habit for a few days, his eyes clear, his own, he is trying to be sweet, he smiles wanly whenever some catastrophe overtakes him, like an actor with no conviction. But someone

else controls his muscles. He is not riding it now but
lives in the beak of something huge and dark that dangles
him just out of my reach.

Our brains are all circuitry; not very imaginative, I
tend to see it blue and red and yellow like the wires in
phones, easier to sort impulses that way. I want to see
inside Christopher's head, I stare viciously though I try
to do it when he's involved with something else. (He
never is, he would feel me a hundred light years behind
him.) I vow never to *study* him again, it's futile anyway,
his forehead's not a one-way mirror. Promises, always
my promises: they are glass. I know when they shat-
ter—no, when he shatters them, throwing something
of value—there will be edges to draw blood, edges
everywhere. He says, "What are you *looking* at all the
time? Bad Christopher the dragon?" He looks wilted,
pathetic, seen-through. But I haven't seen a thing.

"Chrissie." I put my arms around him. He doesn't
want to bruise the air he breathes, maybe we're all
jumbled in his sight. He doesn't read yet, I know that's
why. It's all upside down or somehow mixed together—
cubist sight, is there such a thing? He sees my face and
the top of my head, say, at the same time. Or everything looms at him, quivering like a fun-house mirror,
swollen, then slowly disappears down to a point. He
has to subdue it before it overtakes him? How would
we ever know? Why, if he saw just what we see—the
cool and calm of all the things of the world all sorted
out like laundry ("Oh, Margaret, come off it!") why
would he look so bewildered most of the time like a
terrier being dragged around by his collar, his small
face thrust forward into his own perpetual messes?

He comes to me just for a second, pulling on his tan
windbreaker, already breathing fast to run away somewhere, and while I hold him tight a minute, therapeutic
hug for both of us, he pinches my arm until the purple
capillaries dance with pain.

"Let me take him with me when I go to D.C. next
week." Howard.

I stare at him. "You've got to be kidding."

"No, why would I kid about it? We'll manage, we
can go see some buildings after my conference is out,

go to the Smithsonian. He'd love the giant pendulum."
His eyes are already there in the cool of the great
vaulted room where everything echoes and everything
can break.

I am fascinated by his casualness. "What would he
do all day while you're in your meeting? Friend. My
intrepid friend."

"Oh, we'd manage something. He'd keep busy. Paper
and pencil . . . ."

"*Howie*." Am I crazy? Is he? Do we live in the
same house?

He comes and takes both my hands. There is that
slightly conniving look my husband gets that makes me
forget, goddammit, why I married him. He is all too
reasonable and gentle a man most of the time, but this
look is way in the back of his eyes behind a pillar,
peeking out. I feel surrounded. "You can't take him."
I wrench my hands away.

"Maggie—" and he tries to take them again, bungler,
as though they're contested property.

"I forbid it. Insanity. You'll end up crushing him to
death to get a little peace! I know."

He smiles with unbearable patience. "I know how
to handle my son."

But I walk out of the room, thin-lipped, taking a
bowl of fruit to the children, who are raging around,
both of them, in front of the grade-A educational television that's raging back.

The next week Howie goes to Washington and we
all go to the airport to see him off. I don't know what
Howard told him but while Jody sleeps Christopher
cries noisily in the back of the car and flings himself
around so wildly, like a caged bear, that I have to stop
the car on the highway shoulder and buckle him into
his seat belt. "You will walk home," I threaten, calm
because I can see the battle plan. He's got a little of
his father in him; that should make me feel better.

He hisses at me and goes on crying, forcing the tears
and walloping the back of my seat with his feet the
whole way home.

Log: The long long walk to school. A block and a
half. Most of the kids in the kindergarten with Chris-

topher walk past our house alone, solidly bearing straight
west with the bland eight-o'clock sun at their backs.
They concentrate, they have been told not to cross
heavy traffic alone, not to speak to strangers, not to
dawdle. All the major wisdom of motherhood pinned
to their jackets like a permission slip. Little orders
turning into habits and hardening slowly to superego:
an amber that holds commands forever. Christopher
lacks it the way some children are born without a crucial
body chemical. Therefore, I walk him to school every
day, rain or shine, awake or asleep.

Jody's in her stroller slouching. She'd rather be home.
So would I. It's beginning to get chilly out, edgy, and
that means the neighborhood's been stripped of summer
and fall, as surely as if a man came by one day confis-
cating color. What little there is, you wouldn't think it
could matter. Blame the mayor. The window boxes are
crowded with brown stringy corpses, like tall crab grass.
Our noble pint-sized trees have shrunk back into themselves, they lose five years in winter. Fontaine, always
improving his property, has painted his new brick wall
silver over the weekend—it has a sepulchral gleam in
the vague sunlight, twinkling as placidly as a woman
who's come in sequins to a business meeting, *believ-
ing* in herself. Bless him. Across from us the Rosenbergs have bought subtle aged wood shutters, they look
like some dissected Vermont barn door, and a big rustic
barrel that will stand achingly empty all winter, weighted
with a hundred pounds of dirt to exhaust the barrel
burglars. I wonder what my illusions look like through
the front window.

Christopher's off and running. "Not in the street!"
I get so tired of my voice, especially because I know
he doesn't hear it. "Stay on the curb, Christopher."
There's enough damage to be done there. He is swinging on that new couple's gate, straining the hinges,
trying to fan up a good wind; then, when I look up
from attending to Jody's dropped and splintered Ritz
cracker, he's gone—clapping together two garbage-
can lids across the street. Always under an old lady's
window, though with no particular joy—his job, it's
there to be done. Jody is left with her stroller braked
against a tree for safe keeping while I retrieve him. No

one ever told me I'd grow up to be a shepherdess; and bad at it too—undone by a single sheep.

We are somehow at the corner, at least I can demand he hold my hand and drag us across the street where the crossing guard stands and winks at me daily, as dependably as a blinking light. She is a good lady, Mrs. Cortes, from a couple of blocks down in the Projects, with many matching daughters, one son, Anibal, on the sixth-grade honor roll and another on Riker's Island, a junkie. She is waving cars and people forward in waves, demonstrating "community involvement" to placate the gods who are seeing to Anibal's future, I know it. I recognize something deep behind her lively eyes, sunk there: a certain desperate casualness while the world has its way with her children. Another shepherdess without a chance. I give her my little salute.

By now, my feet heavy with the monotony of this trip, we are on the long school block. The barbed wire of the playground breaks for the entrance halfway down. This street, unlived on, is an unrelenting tangle—no one ever sees the generous souls who bequeath their dead cars to the children, but there are dozens, in various stages of decay; they must make regular deliveries. Christopher's castles; creative playthings, and broken already so he never gets blamed. For some reason he picks the third one. He's already in there, across a moat of broken windshield glass, reaching for the steering wheel. The back seat's burned out, the better to jump on. All the chrome has been cannibalized by the adults—everything that twists or lifts off, leaving a carcass of flung bones, its tin flesh dangling.

"Christopher, you are late and I. Am. Not. Waiting." But he will not come that way. My son demands the laying-on of hands. Before I can maneuver my way in, feeling middle-aged and worrying about my skirt, hiked up over my rear, he is tussling not with one boy but with two. They fight over nothing—just lock hands and wrestle as a kind of greeting. "I break the muh-fuh's head," one announces matter-of-factly—second grader maybe. Christopher doesn't fight for stakes like that, though. Whoever wants his head can have it, he's fighting to get his hands on something, keep them warm. I am reaching over the jagged door, which is split in two and full of rain water. The school bell rings, that raspy grinding, and the two boys, with a whoop, leap over the downed windshield and are gone. Christopher is grater-scraped along one cheek but we have arrived more or less in one piece.

I decide I'd better come in with him and see to it his cheek is washed off. He is, of course, long gone by the time I park the stroller and take the baby out. He never bothers to say good-by. Maybe six-year-olds don't.

I pull open the heavy door to P.S. 193. It comes reluctantly, like it's in many parts. These doors are not for children. But then, neither is the school. It's a fairly new building but the 1939 World's Fair architecture has just about caught up with the lobby—those heavy streamlined effects. A ship, that's what it looks like; a dated ocean liner, or the lobby of Rockefeller Center, one humble corner of it. What do the kids see, I wonder? Not grandeur.

There's a big lit-up case to the left that shows off sparse student pieties, untouchable as seven-layer cakes at the bakery. THIS LAND IS *YOUR* LAND, THIS LAND IS *MY* LAND. Every figure in the pictures, brown, black, dead-white (blank), mustard yellow, tulip red, and olive green (who's that?), is connected more or less at the wrist, like uncut paper dolls (HANDS ACROSS THE SEA). The whole world's afraid to drop hands, the hell with summit talks, SALT talks, we're on the buddy system. Well, *they* go up and down the halls irrevocably linked so, their lips sealed, the key thrown over their endless shoulder, only the teacher nattering on and on about discipline and respect, wearing heels that must sound like SS boots, though they are intended merely to mean business. Christopher tells me only that his teachers are noisy and hurt his ears; he does not bother to specify how.

And what he sees when he puts his thin shoulder to the door at eight-thirty and heaves? He probably catches that glaring unnecessary shine on the floor, an invitation, and takes it. That worried crease between big eyes, his face looks back at him out of deep water. Deeper when he's drugged. So he careens around without ice skates, knocks against other kids hard,

thumps into closed doors, nearly cracks open THIS
LAND IS *YOUR* LAND. He is the wiseacre who dances
to hold the door for his class, then when the last dark
pigtail is through skips off in the wrong direction, leaps
the steps to the gym or the auditorium or whatever lives
down there in deserted silence most of the morning,
the galley of this ship. I don't blame him, of course I
don't, but that isn't the point, is it? I am deprived of
these fashionable rebellious points. We only, madam,
allow those in control to be out of control. As it were.
If you follow. Your son, madam, is not rebelling. He
is unable. Is beyond. Is utterly. Is unthinkable. Catch
him before we do.

We are certainly late, the lines are all gone, the kids
settling into their rooms, their noise dwindling like a
cutback motor. Jody and I just stand for a minute or
two tuning in. Her head is heavy on my shoulder. Already
there's a steady monitor traffic, the officious kids scur-
rying to do their teachers' bidding like tailless mice. I
was one of them for years and years, God, faceless and
obliging, official blackboard eraser (which meant a few
cool solitary minutes just before three each day, down
in the basement storeroom clapping two erasers together,
hard, till they smoked with the day's vanished lessons).
I would hardly have stopped my frantic do-gooding to
give the time of day (off the clocks that jerked forward
with a click every new minute) to the likes of Christopher. I'd have given him a wide berth, I can see myself
going the other way if he were coming toward me in
the narrow hall.

This hall, just like the ones I grew up in except for
the "modernistic" shower tile that reaches halfway up,
has a muted darkened feeling, an underwater thrum.
Even the tile is like the Queens Midtown Tunnel,
deserted. I will not be particularly welcome in Christopher's kindergarten room, there is that beleaguered
proprietary feeling that any parent is a spy or come to
complain. (I, in my own category, have been forbidden
to complain, at least tacitly, having been told that my
son really needs one whole teacher to himself, if not
for his sake, then for the safety of the equipment and
"the consumables," of which he is not one.)

Christopher has disappeared into his class, which—

I see it through the little porthole—is neat and earnest
and not so terribly different from a third-grade room,
say, with its alphabets and exhortations to patriotism
and virtue above eye level. They are allowed to paint
in one color at a time. A few, I see, have graduated to
two; they must be disciplined, promising children in
their securely tied smocks. One spring they will hatch
into monitors. Christopher is undoubtedly banned from
the painting corner. (Classroom economy? Margaret,
your kitchen, your bedroom, your bathroom this morning. Searching for the glass mines hidden between the
tiles.) Mrs. Seabury is inspecting hands. The children
turn them, patty-cake, and step back when she finishes
her scrutiny, which is as grave as a doctor's. Oh Christopher! She has sent him and another little boy to the
sink to scrub; to throw water, that is, and stick their
fingers in the spout in order to shower the children in
the back of the room. I am not going in there to identify
myself.

Mrs. Seabury is the kind of teacher who, with all
her brown and black kids on one side of the room (this
morning in the back, getting showered), talks about
discrimination and means big from little, forward from
backward, ass from elbow. Now I see she has made
Christopher an honorary black child, or maybe one of
your more rambunctious Puerto Ricans. They are all
massed back there for the special inattention of the
aide, who is one of my least favorite people: she is
very young and wears a maxi-skirt that the kids keep
stepping on when she bends down. (Therefore she bends
down as little as possible.) The Future Felons of America and their den mother. I'm caught somewhere between
my first flash of anger and then shame at what I suppose,
wearily, is arrogance. What am I angry at? That he has
attained pariah-hood with them, overcoming his
impeccable WASP heritage in a single leap of adrenalin? Jesus. They are the "unruly characters" he's
supposed to be afraid of: latchkey babies, battered boys
and abused girls, or loved but hungry, scouted by rats
while they sleep. Products of this-and-that converging,
social, political, economic, each little head impaled on
a point of the grid. Christopher? My warm, healthy,
nursed and coddled, vitamin-enriched boy, born on Blue

Cross, swaddled in his grandparents' gifts from Lord & Taylor? What in the hell is our excuse? My pill-popping baby, so sad, so reduced and taken from himself when he's on, so indescribable, air-borne, when he's off. This week he is off; I am sneaking him a favor.

I see him now flapping around in a sort of ragged circle with the other unimaginables, under the passive eye of that aide. Crows? Buzzards? Not pigeons, anyway. They make their own rowdy music. Then Christopher clenches his whole body, I see it coming, and stops short, slamming half a dozen kids together, solid rear-end collisions. It looks like the New Jersey Turnpike, everybody whiplashed, tumbling down. No reason, no why's, there is never anything to explain. Was the room taking off, spinning him dizzy? Was he fending something off, or trying to catch hold? The others turn to him, shout so loud I can hear them out here where I'm locked, underwater—and they all pile on. Oh, can they pile! It's a sport in itself. Feet and hands and dark faces deepening a shade. The aide gets out of the way, picking her skirt out of the rubble of children at her feet.

One heavy dark boy with no wrists finally breaks through the victor: his foot is on Christopher's neck. The little pale face jerks up stiffly, like an executed man's. I turn away. When I make myself turn back the crowd is unraveling as Mrs. Seabury approaches. Faces all around are taking on that half-stricken, half-delighted "uh-oh" look. I was always good at that, one of the leaders of censure and shock. It felt good.

But Christopher sinks down, quiet. She reaches down roughly and yanks his fresh collar. Good boy, he doesn't look up at her. But something is broken. The main-spring, the defiant arch of his back that I would recog-nize, his, mine, I find I am weeping, soundless as everything around me, I feel it suddenly like blood on my cheeks. This teacher, this stranger, and her cohorts have him by his pale limp neck. They are teaching him how to lose; or me how to win. My son is down for the count, breathing comfortably, accommodating, only his fingers twitching fiercely at his sides like gill slits puff-ing, while I stand outside, a baby asleep on my shoul-der. I am the traitor, he sees me through my one-way mirror, and he is right. I am the witch. Every day they walk on his neck, I see that now, but he will never tell me about it. I weep but cannot move.

245

(Migdalia Colon's, third floor rear)

A LETTER TO ISMAEL IN THE GRAVE

Somebody once told me I didn't have welfare mothers' eyes.

I. I. I. I. I. Like white is supposed to be made up of all the colors, I is made up of all the words you can possibly say all running together in a circle very fast. It is red and shiny and purple and sweet. A mouthful of I-berries. Here, have some. I want to put it on the mailbox. Use it for my signature. Frame it and hang it on the wall all gold. Put it between my legs in bed at night. Sing it out in church. Show it around like a fat new baby. It's the best baby we never had, the one I made myself, after the children had gone to bed, just before you died.

You know what your sister said to me, don't you? She says it with her pointy finger. Back to the ashes, Cinderella. Now be a dead man's wife the way you were a lost man's widow.

When I was a kid I once walked across the river on the third rail, right next to the BMT. While I was at it in those days making my mama and grandmama jump like fleas, I married you. But I couldn't do that once, like walking the rail, I had to do it and keep doing it for thirteen years. So I fell in the river, my feet in flames.

Does someone always have to get blamed in this world?

The headline was 2 MORE ADDICT DEATHS IN CITY THIS WEEKEND.

What I read was WIFE SAYS SHE DIDN'T KNOW; SAYS SHE STOPPED KNOWING ANYTHING A LONG TIME AGO. And who gets blamed for that?

You know my friend Nilda. Her husband takes a shot every single day of his life for diabetes, very carefully, so he won't go blind or something, or go crazy. How can it be that another man could use his veins for filthy highways: for alleys, that's what, dark dirty alleys. So they could find you collapsed in the thick black of one of your own ruined veins.

Merciful, merciful. That you died before you had to hock your children's eyes and little toes. Before your pig of a liver killed you instead. Before I sold myself out from under you and cheap, to get money for passage. I am not beautiful, no sir, I know that, but I do not have welfare mothers' eyes. In spite of you.

All right, I said to him. But you know I've got tattoos. Those shadows, those stripes of the el laying over me all these years since you (he, Ismael, my husband!) moved me out there. Look what it had to take to get me to this clean block now, this George Street. You move to the nice green cemetery, breathe it in, the only clean air you ever had, and I come running to my sister Migdalia here where most of the houses are for one family, imagine them rolling around in there with stairs inside their own apartment, and yards behind fences, mine, yours, theirs . . . But I swear we've still got the taste of all that darkness in our soup. You have to look pretty hard even in Brooklyn to find an el that they haven't taken down for scrap iron and firewood but you worked hard on it and found us one. You couldn't get sunstroke over here if they gave you a million for trying. One time I saw the slats across my friend Rita's shoulders when she was standing down there on the stoop. They looked like those fox furs I used to stare at when I was a kid, the whole fox with the flat shiny eyes I always thought were real, and the long dark stringy tails. Didn't you used to wonder if it hurt them, to be dragged around on some rich old lady's back?

He was looking at me the other day when I thought I was alone, sitting in the kitchen trying to think. And he said he never saw a woman who kept right on existing when her man wasn't with her. I guess I've had a lot of practice from you, with me and never with me all at the same time. But Jesus, to be that way! What are we, frogs who need a swamp to croak about?

The kind of thing I've been so busy thinking is, Whose fault were you? But whose fault was the you whose fault you were? There's a girl on the front of the Sun-Maid raisin box holding a box of raisins with a girl on it, holding a box of raisins with a girl on it holding.

Something new, I heard them talking on TV about what's called crimes without victims? Do you think there could be something like victims without crimes? That's what we all could be, even the kids—victims' victims. Don't laugh.

Two people live in a room small enough so their shoulders touch. One day one of them asks, "What's your name?" and it turns out they have the same name. By accident. "Well," one of them says, "maybe we have something in common. What do you like best in the world?" She looks at him all coy and says, "You." She smiles because she thinks that's the right answer. "And what do you like best?" He thinks for a minute and says, "Me." So they fall together. It's a tight circle they can both fit into if they get down on all fours and crawl.

Poor Ismael. When you closed your gorgeous eyes that I envied, there must have been nothing behind them to look at. Just dark: your own closed eyes reflected and reflected.

You said I made the children a wall between us, you even made it seem that was all I had them for. But a wall is something to lean on when you have to lean, and anyway, what holds up a house, a roof overhead, if it isn't walls.

I asked you to leave. I threw you out. I left you. But
I've heard about a kind of snake—this is a *moreno*
belief, I think—that kills you and when it thinks you're
dead it sticks its tail up in your nostrils to make sure
you aren't breathing. If you are, it kills you again.
What you used for a tail and where you went looking
to see if I was still alive—I shouldn't have lay down
dead for you so often.

If I ever loved you, even for a minute, then you were
my fault too. I put a check-mark next to you and it
wouldn't rub off. I said sure. I laughed. I said I'm
behind you here, give me your footprints—even for a
minute. I said we fit.

What did you say to me?

So it's going on. I think of myself, I shine up the me
with powder and pink lips and what do I see but a
roach climbing like a little trooper up from the baseboard, and what do I think of? He is like a genie that
goes in and out of my toilet water bottle but you are
always somewhere around without being called. I paid
money I didn't even have to get you a better place in
the ground than you ever got me up here, and a woman
to say the rosary a full three days, and you're still
smoke around my shoulders. I looked at this fat roach
that never got sick eating the paint off the walls because
there's better things to pick at, and thought how that
was you lying next to me in bed—that bed the man
from welfare used to say was too big for one person
and leer at me—and that is still you lying in darker
dark and a roach might be taking away your fingers
right now for all I know. For all you know.

I know something you don't know.

The priest keeps saying, spreading out his big sweaty
hands to calm me down, Now Ismael knows the last
great secret, he is luckier than we are. Then he goes
and names all the saints whose faces you're getting to
see whether you want to or not. But I saw you dying
and it was like watching you do something very very

private when you didn't see me looking.

It wasn't merciful, I lied, something just got sucked away out of your eyes and when it was gone your cheeks began to collapse fast. But it was more of you than you ever showed me, dressed or naked, cold or hot, sick or sober. It was more.

Now how do I get out from under you? That's what I mean, I'm like one of those women a man died while he was inside of. Had a heart attack or something, you've heard about that. No matter where they take his body, she must always see his shoulders hunkering over her with his eyes wide on her face. I know it. And she thinks it's her fault too, a little bit, somehow a shadow of the fault, a sniff, a turn, an ooze of the fault.

The night he came home with me the first time and the last, Rosa who is your daughter no matter who's in my bed, came running into the bedroom crying Daddy is a ghost and he's scaring me. He tried to comfort her but she didn't even know who he was sitting there wrapped up in a sheet, and it took me an hour to get her back to bed. Then all we wanted to do was forget we ever saw each other, and he got dressed and went home. And I was glad. If you didn't get Rosa up out of her bed to come running in there on me just in the nick of time, then I think I did, with some strong part of my brain that I can't see.

I was planning another getaway when you escaped. Rosa was at my mother's and Pablo was in his first week of sleep-away camp, and I was going out and get a job, I thought something on a boat going somewhere out of Brooklyn, I don't know, but I was standing right at the threshold, in a way. Singing, singing the whole day how you weren't going to lock me up from myself the way you locked me up from you. Then they came and told me they found you, and these little sunbursts of color kept popping in front of my eyes just like when I drink, dark with rainbow colors. They had to lead me. They told me as though it was no secret how you'd been robbing me and telling me stories and laughing at me and shooting your children's groceries up in your arm and my breasts turned to clean round skulls that you had kissed in the morning. Somebody, Julio, said he was surprised I cared so much, I looked so weak choking on my own blood, and he took me to the hospital to breathe in the dead air you breathed out, and I said I don't like to be made a damn fool of, that's all. And there you were turned inside out in your skin like one of your own empty pockets and who was the damn fool then? Julio, the last time I saw him maybe a month ago, ran his hand down my behind with his finger pointing like an arrow, and I thought for a second that I might be free of you. I will tell you without shame I'd like to have made a bow bent for your dear friend Julio's arrow. But after he took me to your sweaty bed and showed you to me stretched out hot with your brain dissolving right before my eyes, I told him to go away. He shames me with myself.

They took you to the morgue and I had to go and check you out like some lost package. I was right there when you died and the doctor knew who I was and you didn't have to die in the street but maybe I do have welfare mothers' eyes. So I traded them down at that place, the morgue: They gave me what was left of you and I gave them my feet and they locked them in a vault.

Now you see——a widow is a dry well. You always hear the opposite. But I'll have them too, won't I? Heart's beetles. Six fat maggots feasting on my tongue that knew your tongue. I. I. I the stillborn.

Ismael. I wish you were alive, I wish, I wish, so I could hate you and get on with it.

251

(basement)

PACO, DREAMING

They are all asleep: Isabel and Paco and Luz and Faye, Junior, Tracy and Nando, her sister Cherry's daughter, Yvonne; also Chico, father of the last three. Plus two dogs, whose sides rise and fall luxuriously where they lie on their sides, looking shot down in their tracks. Do the fish sleep at the top of the water? (About once a week, Junior tries to surprise them asleep but he brings along an army of feet and unstoppable mouths in his wake.)

Ines is awake. She is wearing a blue duster and fancy slippers with a pompom on top but she is working at her noon pace, rolling the dough, turning the meat and olives and peppers for the pastilles, getting the paper ready to dress them in. It is one-thirty. An hour ago she turned down the radio experimentally, then craned her neck toward the middle room where her husband sleeps, and Nando and, tonight, Yvonne in blankets on the floor and—one bed snapped and whined—clicked it off. She is humming. The fluorescent ring makes a dim insect sound.

Ines is small and charged and adept at certain economies of movement. As she cuts she turns the onion neatly under her hand and reaches for the next as she sweeps the pieces off the board into a plastic bowl. Her mouth has a set to it, a smile either just appearing or just fading. Way in the back one of the three in the boys' room shouts out a single word twice; she straightens, listens, frowning. But quiet comes down again. The house is bewitched as if there's been a snowfall through the low lumpy kitchen roof. Mrs. McTave and her skinny daughter turned to clouds of snowflakes settling on her linoleum! All the chrome and the gilt of

the frame around Jesus, around two cats in polka-dot
bows, the china switchplate covers, the slick waxed
floor—all the shine of that whole nice inventory disappearing under a powder of 10X sugar snow. . . . Ines,
smiling, takes the meat to the blender. She shakes her
head and widens her eyes to wake them up, just as she
would if she were skeptical about something, pauses a
moment, then picks up her pace again.

The whole thing goes into the blender, the top clicks
into its slot and she turns it on, shuddering at the shock
of sound, its jungle screech. She scrapes it out and fills
the blender jar again, then once again, glancing over
her shoulder toward the bedrooms. The blades slow
and fail; she shakes it once on its stand, then pries up
the top and pokes her hand in, gets the stuck pieces out
of the way, closes it again, stands patiently watching.
Empties, fills, opens the cap, darts her fingers in, then
widens her eyes all the way to her hairline and makes
a little muffled sound, almost like fierce approval. She
gropes for the switch with her other hand.

The blood is everywhere: on the cabinets she's just
finished scrubbing, in the mash of meat that stands in
the green potato chip bowl, on her duster. She looks
hard at that, the large circles at the top dwindling down
to spots striped and wandering like tears at the hem.
On her robe rusty brown but on the walls an extraordinary healthy red.

Ines is holding her fingers in front of her face, dripping downwards. She looks slightly puzzled, as if they
belong to someone else. She wraps her duster pocket
tightly around her hand and looks around the room like
someone trapped, the doors suddenly hidden behind
trick furniture.

Then she hurries through her husband's stone-silent
room.

Down in the lot way over Wyckoff Street, or Butler.
There's the ASPCA with cages out back and a lot of
noise like they're hurting the animals in there. Where
they brought their first dog when he got hit. Do they
do experiments, a dog is held up on hooks by the
throat. The watchman, whatever he is, that very black

man, gray-black, has his clothes all off, he walks between the cages, his dong bouncing, the little kittens coming up sniffing it, crowding him. Is he the one who planted the crazy garden across the street next to the water works, he goes slowly over the cobblestones, barefoot, up to the chain-link fence, and looks in. All kinds of stuff, whatever it is, stands up straight as fakes: red, yellow, purple and billions of petals. He's got a skinny rear end for an old man, no, but he's not old. He turns his face, it's Pa, not Pa but Ma's husband, that Papi. He's standing in the garden like a hydrant.

Walking down by the Canal, gray, underground gray, chipped stone, soggy cartons, beer cans like a second garden of glass. Right up at the edge looking over stones there's a Baggie in the mud. Picks it up, it's tied with one of those red twist-ems, upside down, fingers fall out of the bag. Knuckles, upper and lower. Whole hands. Toes, Elbows? There are rings, the phony zircon kind, one Mason ring with the secret stuff on it, and one fresh Band-Aid on a thumb. Stuffs them back. Puts it in his pocket like it was just any old thing. Washing for bed sees his right hand up in the bathroom mirror, all its short brown fingers, counts them—they are going about their business like ants. How do fingers get in trouble? Who would punish a toe? A toe with corns? He feels a heavy sadness right in his dream. He vows to his wrists and ankles, out loud, never to mention the Baggie, and the promise is real, he pushes against his sleep with it, and if ever the time comes they go, he goes too.

"Wake up, *please*, Paco. Please get out of there, you got to help me." Shaking him back and forth. "Come on, I think I lost my hand."

"Jesus!" It's wet where she's touching him.

"Come on. Come in the kitchen quick."

"Ma, what did you do—" She is trying to put her other hand over his mouth, he feels it dully in the dark. He hurries along obediently, stubs his toe on the chair in his stepfather's room, but keeps his mouth shut. The kitchen light is like a whip across his face.

"Ma" is all he can say, looking at the blood splashed

all over everything like the red that time when the beets
exploded in the pressure cooker. He doesn't want to
look at her hand that she's holding like a kitten or
something, lightly, in the front of her old robe. She is
very white and the puffs just starting under her deep
eyes anyway are like purple bruises. She looks like a
very little girl, like Luz, with a deflated old face. He
puts his arms around her, not feeling awkward, only
helpless and angry. As though she got into something
she shouldn't have without his permission.

"You got to stop that blood," he announces, trying
to think of something to do it with. "What do they say
about cutting off the pressure or something?" He had
to take a hygiene class in first-term high school, but
you never remember what you need, only names like
Pasteur and the guy that invented the silver bullet.

She shrugs, she is in his hands, looking a little dreamy.
He hopes she's not going to faint. "Sit down, Ma, let
me think." But he can't think, so he says, "Hold it as
tight as you can, let's just get to the hospital."

She sits with a funny little smile.

"What's the matter?"

"Paco?" Her voice singsongs, in no hurry. If it was
him bleeding she'd be out the door ten minutes by now.
She laughs. "I think my fingers are still in the blender."

He is furious and wants to shout and stamp, wake
everybody, grab Papi, get the kids, everybody sort of
huddling around could protect her. Upstairs the McTave
bastards must be snoring up a storm, they could help.
He feels deserted, run out on. He and his mother, who
isn't going to say it hurts, just go off her head quiet,
and they're sleeping.

"What were you *doing?*"

She waves her other hand at him. "Now's no time,
sonny. Making pastilles for the weekend." Laughs.
What a time. "Hey, think about finding a couple
knuckles in your lunch." Her old good laugh like water
that has gravel at the bottom.

"Here, put your coat on," he whispers, grabbing his
windbreaker, his voice thick. It takes a long time to get
her hand through that sleeve.

"Shouldn't we tell Papi?" he says suddenly, as he
unsticks the front door, quietly, with urgent care. What,

are they sneaking out someplace, thick red blood all over the goddamn walls? It'll look like somebody got murdered.

She shakes her head passionately. "It's okay, he won't wake up." The black curls make a little windy sound as they bob against each other.

They don't say a word to each other the whole long block to the hospital. Their heads are down against the shoving cold, and he has his arm around her shoulder like a vise.

It's a good place to go for emergencies: an unpopular hospital. Everybody else who got cut up or was dropping babies or whatever people do at two in the morning, O.D., were all over at the big city hospital where the ambulances took them sure as subways. If this wasn't on your block you wouldn't even know about it, Mary out front holding the ball of the world in a bright blue light. He only guessed they had an emergency room, but that's the first thing a hospital is for, right? That's how they get half their customers.

He feels very proud helping her in the swinging door, talking up for her at the desk, name, address, age, she's so young it's somehow like a compliment to him. But he has to stay in the dim waiting room while they go off with her, a nun holding her arm. Teetering a little in her fancy bedroom slippers. He wonders if the nun objects to the way she's dressed.

It's a long time, in bad light, with nothing but health magazines around, prevent this, augment that, and *The Catholic Home Messenger*. He closes his eyes and sees naked girls in the boy's gym, climbing the ropes, doing flips on the old battered horses he uses, and one particular girl in his algebra class sitting behind her desk smiling with her breasts in her hands like presents she's giving him. Like Mary out there holding up two worlds as round and brown as basketballs. She's darker than his mother and her teeth are pretty bad but the rest of her always gets in the way of his equations. It's strange to watch the nuns walking up to the desk and back, soundless as the TV with the sound turned down, thinking about that girl with her hands full of herself.

Paco closes his eyes again. Once he saw the pistol

Papi got out of hock. First he showed it to her, then he waved it at her and left with only a tee shirt on and was gone how long? Forever. She acted like it was. Didn't put on make-up till he was back at the door, then she ran to get her lipstick and silver eye stuff. A week or two. Then there was the time, just when he had to be here to take the exam for the special high schools, when she suddenly flung a bunch of clothes in a suitcase and took all of them out to Cherry's house in Jersey, where it stank worse than it does in Red Hook by the shipyards. So now he goes to John Jay, a four-year prison term, no parole for good behavior. Whatever the hell they were fighting about and he gets punished. And Chico, Papi, puts too damn much money in that car of his, everybody says it (and then blames him because it's never working), his *comadre* likes to say it to his face, daring him. And too much time, you like it better than you like her, you don't deserve a good wife who stays home nights, cooks you *two* kinds of rice, *bendito*, your yellow, your white, you make her take turns just so she can't serve you last night's rice! Who'd want her, Papi, not his Pa, would say, sneering, old bitch, the worn-out shoe with her seven kids. Once he said to Uncle Fredo, "Nothin' left of her, no tread, you should see, it's like sticken' it up in Grand Central Station." Then he looked and saw Paco listening and, man to man, winked. But when he ran out on her she went around looking about the color of the white rice, like she was going to just stop one morning and not be able to get out of bed. Maybe it still feels good to her, even if he calls her insides bad names. He never caught her talking about Papi, except with a hurt face. Once only she had said to him, "You don't remember your father." No, he didn't. "Well, don't say nothing about Chico then. There are all kinds of men and some cut deeper than others." He got the feeling he wasn't supposed to ask any questions. The one thing about Chico that was good, he supposed, was how he insisted all her children were his too, especially when he was drunk. Which meant he could knock them around, order them, shame them, ignore them. That was something anyway, but then one time she threw it up to him and said, "Leave them alone, get off them all. You got your own kids." His other ones, and Nando, Tracy, Luz. Paco wondered if he would understand women by the time he had one of his own.

She comes out looking like herself again, finally, smiling thanks at the doctor, flirting a little, showing teeth he never gets to see. She chatters all the way home, the way she would after a great event, a picnic or a christening, nervous only now that it's over and her hand looms in front of her, huge and padded.

"You look like you could use a boxing glove," he says. He needs to join her, make it nothing at all.

"I could manage with a couple less knuckles," she says, elated. "The doctor told me I was lucky I didn't do no worse." In the gray wash of the street light she looks satisfied.

When the door to the basement is shut as quietly as he'd opened it, he helps her sponge up the kitchen. He looks away as the brown water comes spattering down into the drain. She can't wring out her sponge with one hand but she tries anyway, bearing down against the sink bottom. He tells her to cut it out. They shake with held laughter, she with her triple-sized paw stuffed in her mouth as a silencer. The live color is back in her cheeks.

Finally as he is straightening the last chair—it looks as though there's been a fight, a sort of playful fist-fight, maybe—she comes over and puts her soft arms around him. "My Paco," she says, not quite to him. "My little *machito*." His head is bent as though he's apologizing, and all he can do is smell her, half sweat, half Avon Topaze Papi gave her for Christmas.

254

(upper duplex)

MUSTARD SEED

The baby is in her carriage for the first time. Under her fist-tight head is a fancy pillow-slip, lace all around, with a satin stripe like Miss America's, announcing her name before anyone asks. It is not Molly Dungan's style, rather a gift of her mother, whose way of making the best of things tends toward the grandiose in exact proportion to her misery.

Molly looks at her baby and thinks again, Yes, a child can come as though by parcel post. A knock at the door, she's yours, given like a gift. Fairy tales are full of that, children delivered from hand to hand, prizes, forfeits, always someone's to give . . . She has signed a paper that says I am sane. *Promises* I am sane (which in the first place is not sane). Says I will apportion my moneys into two piles, a small one for myself, a tall one for this child's shoes and cereal. It's a contract, she thinks, stamped, sealed and filed somewhere, and I have married a daughter.

Whom no one would marry. Or rather, whom someone married and then, taking a long long time about it, gave a second thought to and began to itch all over (in a manner of speaking). Molly is maneuvering the carriage through the narrow inner door, thinking of the back of Verne's head. How deadly the fit of his head to his neck, as though someone had tried to do a complicated joining job with too few screws. The first time she came near him from behind and touched his shoulder, he had jumped. It made her feel good, charged in a way she wasn't at all used to. "Your neck looks so tense," she had said shyly, feeling a tentative need to bend and unbend her fingers, the way they feel when she approaches a breadboard full of dough waiting to

be worked to smoothness. That was the way everything
had felt with Verne: new energy that she had only
dreamed of, glimpsing it in others, had moved jerkily
through the channels she had always suspected were
there. There were no huge surges of desire, no flashing
insights and sudden weakness; better, since she was a
skeptical woman, and seasoned in her skepticism, not
that young, a solid two-footed resounding weight of
certainty. Yes this is good, it is right. This sober man
makes sense to me. So she had said quietly, seductively
(but he could ignore the seductiveness without embar-
rassing her, she played it that safe), "Your neck looks
so tense, can I massage it for you? Help it relax a
little?"

Verne, poor Verne, all strung together with catgut
and chicken wire. He had moved his chin warily, cock-
ing it all the more tensely to challenge her. But she was
standing so close to him that he must have felt the
waves of hopeful warmth coming off her flowered
shirtwaist. He bowed his head and she laid hands on
his flesh, swarthy and firm right under the close-cropped
hair. (All this was a few years ago when hair had to be
banked neatly in back—when she cut it for him, their
little economy, it was all but impossible to do it well.
Now, last time she saw him, he was his short-haired
self under such a weight of longish hair she might have
thought it a wig. If he were a different man.) So,
misleading her, he had done this sort of thing: she
kneaded and pressed, she patted and prodded, all the
way down his resistant shoulders and back, and she
had felt his constant, persistent tension disintegrate.
The tendons or whatever they were, muscles? softened
and then the slackness of his back was full in her hands
as though she had subdued it. Verne had eased himself
around slowly so that she was in the crook of his arm
finally and had kissed her with his hard mouth. He hurt
her so often with his mouth, not out of unappeasable
passion but with that same insistent tautness that couldn't
really feel her there. His kisses were more teeth than
tongue. Because he was just so much less hard than a
stone she could soften him into her arms, but look.
Molly, look, she finally had to say to herself, what you
love in him is what *you* can do to him, against such

odds. How you cozy him (briefly) into human positions. How you can feel like a woman who sings and smiles sleepily with your hair across the pillow, who can make him feel or pretend to feel he needs you. What you love is you, for want of him. She had married a man with a ramrod up his ass. Once upon a time, before she met him, she would not have said "ass." Now that there is color in her speech and in her clothes she would say it, and more, but that irony didn't make it any less of a ramrod.

Molly is pushing the carriage through the front door. She gets the front wheels down the doorstep onto the welcome mat and stops. Good God, how do you get a carriage down the steps with a baby in it? She had arranged Carie Lyn so carefully, as though for an ocean voyage. She looks around, flushing, to see if anyone has been watching. All the women on this block who were born to this.

Molly has fair skin, freckled like a lawn full of clover. It prickles now, carbonated. She is about to think the worst thought she knows, it gathers in her exactly as her migraines do, a twitch of imminence before she even knows it's there. She is pushing it away almost with her hands, her breath held, averting her eyes from herself as the quick dumb tears press forward. Who says, who says, any other mother would know (it breaks through, a shout of pain) would know better? How would she know, any other, any real, how will I do this, this is not my baby who ended in a bottle, what difference does it make whose baby, she walked out holding him (the ones who don't make it, the nurse said, are more often hims) stiffly away from her white cotton cleanness like something unclean, unnatural as the pain, in a labeled jar my bulbous clot of a child, unchild, the best in me purple, blue, brown, red, like something that exploded. Where do they bury the little yolks that are not even corpses, do they burn them back to ash-flecks the size of sperm and egg, or flush them down, or chop them up in a bowl? She asked and the nurse, making out the death certificate in her name, patted her arm as though she were insane.

She turns her close-cropped head against the door frame but does not remove her hand from the cool

carriage handle. Her tears seem to make their way like
an underground spring up through inches of dirt, the
rigid silence she has enforced on herself since Verne
made her weep that one last time, turning his purie-
marble eyes on her. "No we will not, no, what the
stinking world does not need is a child who smells like
we do. You and me, separately and together." Did he
celebrate the death, the non-life of that one, then? Did
he wish it? *Did he cause it?* Were all the children of
his stone body stone? Or was she, old flesh, just past
its prime, so rotten inside she could not warm anything
growing there but her own death?

Molly jerks the carriage up the doorstep again, brakes
it, very carefully lifts the baby out, Carie Lyn Dugan
swathed in the softest pink and white blankets, and—
suddenly casual—rests the bundle on the hall floor,
sleeping face up, and rackets the carriage down the
cement steps, one-two-three. She marches back, picks
up the baby, who stirs with a comfortable moan, and
before she has blinked her eyes open, has her deep
under the carriage hood again, the CARIE LYN pillow
("Really dear," her mother had said, seizing on a focus
for her disapproval, "they had to special-order this!
Couldn't you have picked a more everyday name?"
Always different, Molly, is what she was thinking, of
course; always up your own tree, alone) pressed to the
back, all sweet sixteen ruffles flapping down George
Street. Sometimes these days, mood alternating with
mood, she frightens herself a little. It is like living
with a stranger.

The carriage takes some getting used to. It makes
unwieldy turns and overcomes curbs with an effort; she
needs to learn various subtle pressures of the heel of
her hand, wheels-up wheels-down maneuvers. Teaching French to indifferent fifteen-year-olds is easier, she
thinks, and this time smiles.

She is waiting for a green light, standing between a
man and a woman, and color creeps to the top of her
cheekbones. She's heard her friends talk about the
embarrassment of walking down the street for the first
time in a maternity dress—what is it, the night-secrets
you are giving away, or the way your private image of

yourself hasn't begun to catch up with the single public image you've become? The woman turns to look at her absently, and her pink powdered face softens at the sight of the carriage, a mouthful of sugar gathering behind puckery lips. Molly stands very straight, the way she does when a truck-driver toots his horn and whistles, looking hard at the light as though it might dare to change unnoticed.

She must look like a nursemaid walking someone else's child. A little oldish for the young mother's stance. Dry skin, creases bannering out from the corners of her eyes, a rack of bones at the shoulders of her sundress. Slender or skinny, neat or parsimonious, brightly dressed in an orange and purple cotton, or desperately ingénue? But of course she was even thinner at seventeen—there is some settling of firmness, gravity's if not her own, to make her less transparent now. And, wanting to be invisible, her clothes ten, fifteen years ago were always gray or brown, thrift-shop style. But no woman a good few years over thirty should be alone unless she has a very firm view of herself or she will falter terribly (she's thought this more and more) between a cool view of what she is and a fevered view of what she's always wanted to be. . . .

An absurdity. Molly Fry Dugan, B.A., M.A., French with honors, divorcee, WASP, dreamer of adolescent dreams, keeper of her own body, gratefully knowing it is in better hands now than it has ever been before, her canvas shoes on large feet, her long legs attached to a pale and hollow trunk that no one seems much inclined to want to come near or look at in light or darkness (Verne having said that her small wan nipples were like owls' eyes, sad and round and too lonely to be helped)— that Molly Dugan is wheeling, jerkily, a borrowed carriage with (it is becoming apparent) an incipient squeak; the carriage containing the delicious curled body, all new cells, some never sloughed yet! of the baby she found by irrevocable legal means in a basket one day at her body's closed gates. An absurdity.

She is walking in a fog of humiliation, bumping into the dangling carriage basket every few steps, she is so out of phase with her own stride. This is not the way things were supposed to be! It is all falling apart, fall-

ing down, ashes, ashes, can she keep the baby alive a
day? It awes her that people, teen-agers even, who
can't pass her French exams, seem to manage to keep
such tender bones attached. Can you be mortified before
yourself? Yes, she sees it, if you spend enough time
alone, you make a good enough audience and judge.
She wants to go and cry behind a tree, like a kid who
has to pee.

No trail blazer, ladies and gentlemen, no historic
landmark case, whose name was not in the evening
edition, hardly the first single woman in the state of
New York to be allowed to adopt a baby alone, still she
is standing on Atlantic Avenue, corner Fowler Street,
covering her prickling eyes with her hands, having
forgotten how to set one foot before the other. She is
flushed, sweat pokes down between her unuseful breasts.
At a standstill, swaying, her face is in her hands.

There is no one in the world who can tell her anything
she needs to know. Every problem from here on in is
her own. Alone up her own tree. Right, Mama. Right
again. Her friends are so put off by her "strength" she
can barely talk to them, she has put such distance
between herself and their conventional lives that the
more they admire her the more she understands how
much they'd been pitying her all this time. Her parents
are too angry at her, underneath their cowed silence,
to say a single word. Not even congratulations or good
luck, which, though unhelpful, as though she were
launching a yacht, would at least have been a sign of
hope and reconciliation. Just that presents arrive, cold
in their white frothy wrappings: some kind of peace
gesture easy for her mother, the way she's seen food
standing cooling on the table between certain friends
and their parents. Demilitarized zone.

Carie is stirring, protesting because the carriage has
stopped. She is thrusting her head from side to side
like a turtle. She has, or will have, the head of a little
blackberry. Though the hair is still thin there are very
tight shiny curls laid one above the other, blue-black,
purple-black. Her skin, a light pinky-brown when she
was born, is darkening now day by day; at the folds of
her elbows, behind her knees, the places her mother
drips the tickly water from her cloth, for fun, she is

very dark, graying toward black, just as you might
expect in shadowy places. Molly is not dismayed at
how much browner she is turning, but she feels guilt
in exchange for her curiosity: Who is this stranger?
(Hey lady, she is your daughter. We hereby give her to
you because she is—even to you who intend to love
her—strange, if not ugly. To the state she is worthless,
less even. A burden. Therefore she is yours for the
asking. If you can give her some worth, fine [though
not so much it will ever come home to the state to
roost]. And keep the little bastard off the welfare rolls,
will you?)

So Molly begins to move again. Fowler has narrowed
by now, near the Projects, and gotten a bit patchy, and
the carriage rides the waves of broken sidewalk like a
small ship. Every now and then she rams the front
wheels against a protruding square and it nearly bounces
out of her hands. It's a bad time of day to be walking
here—school must just be over and the sidewalk is
awash with teen-agers. This end of the street the stores
are random and grubby, many of indeterminate nature,
every face is black, and the children are exuberantly at
home. Girls go past her in clots calling out to their
friends walking across the street. Most of them are
clutching their notebooks to their chests in that crook-
armed protective hug no boy has ever needed. She
feels herself in a jungle of legs, long legs and such
high asses, and all sharply dressed in the tiny skirts
and ponchos and overalls-tops of the exact moment.
These girls, that boy flashing past in his rust-colored
pants, running—outrageously right on him, with gold
moving fast down the sides like racing stripes—some
of them have such distinctive features and figures you
know you could find their mother-tribes in Africa, they
could go join hands with their ancestors and show their
inheritance around, these great-great-grandchildren.
(Why was that—when you've found a child's eyes in
her mother or his height in his father, you feel you've
found the source. But when you see the miraculous
construction of bones on some black children, back
you go to their lost tribe, why? As though their only
real parents were free, the lucky ones who never saw a
slave ship?)

Carie Lyn, what will she look like, the young women from Kinshasa, from the Ivory Coast? Will she be short and round, yielding early to fat no matter what spinach her mother feeds her? Or will she have those narrow wire legs that bend and straighten and bend again they are so endless, and her little rear tucked way up tight and sassy? Verne had once told her—her good liberal decent math-teacher husband from Fond du Lac, Wisconsin—that girls who looked like that were all chippies (his word: a little cuter than he meant, but he liked to hide from threats. He must have had one once). Maybe they would meet again in fifteen years and Verne would have to think, Molly has raised this little whore, well, could that really be? Maybe he would reconsider his certainty about narrow long-legged black girls. Maybe, more likely, he would think it made a lot of sense, yes, Molly, who had so lustfully prodded him into her bed, guilty of his guilt. But walking on this street among these girls and their noisy boyfriends, she feels neutered, pathetic in their eyes. Not a soul has noticed her but she is holding firm to the slick bar of the carriage, slowed, waiting for them to blow past like a summer shower.

Carie Lyn blinks, her eyes open. They are still look-ing inward. Gross shadows draw them but not Molly's smile, yet, not the tumult of her people, anyone's people, on Fowler Street. The mother who bore her—her other mother? her real? her unreal?—was a few, but not so many, years older than these high school girls. Her father might have been anyone, no record will ever bear his name: he was a magic wand indifferent (presumably) to its power. Would they be angry if they knew their daughter was going to grow up in a white lady French teacher's duplex, with soulless food and pottery on the shelves, Mozart on the phonograph? Their daughter? But there is no such person, there *is* no "they." Her skin is a question of physical substance, pigment, her culture a matter of chance. A baby this new lies in the light of her beholder's eye.

Boring! Boring! She's been through all this a hundred times. Still, when Molly sees two young men making good time down the block toward her, one in a blue dashiki, one in a gorgeous robe that seems to have caught the glow of some sun setting, she tenses, her freckles drowned in a flush. They near her, both have hair that stands out all around electrified, and eyes focused keenly on something. She is knocked down, in her mind, she should be, her baby snatched and carried away under the extravagant robe, and she is left without a word in her mouth. Give our sister a home, a name? What, you still get to own slaves? You get to steal our children, come back to show them off in lace with your name on them?

They had barely talked about any of this when she held her stiff and proper discussions with the agency. So little that was real had dared to sit between them in those social sessions, they had been more like teas with her maiden aunts on their porches in Old Lyme than legal confrontations. The point was (there might just as well have been a notice on the wall commanding it in the name of the governor) she was to be all petitioning gratitude and maternal anticipation, and they the bountiful horn out of whose miraculous mouth her child was born to her. The Miriam Waddington Home As Cornucopia. Her particular fears did not appear in the pamphlets they were constantly handing her; those dealt with laughably remote questions like "Should we tell our child that he is adopted?" and "How much does resemblance matter—if we are blond, should our child be blond?" To discuss her guilt in the face of men in dashikis would have been to bring a family of slime-green frogs to the conferences and set them free on the interviewer's glass-topped desk. To say, yes, they are right! I know they are!—and who, in this fairy tale, would have won this child (f., blk.)?

She is back on George Street, the numbers way up. This is one of those cruel streets, like Park Avenue, that likes to rub your nose in the stink of its differences. Good fortune, bad fortune, all say "George." The 200 block, her own and Carie's, is the one the realtors call "the ice-cream block." Every new gas lamp makes them gloat. Its sweetness makes her stomach sink. This, now, is a block of small factories and broken driveways, and a coffee-packing plant that sends out a sharp, bitter, very brown smell, almost like dark woods full of mushrooms. She pushes the carriage up

to a stuccoed wall. Across the street, for no apparent
reason, is a bench with an Alpo dog-food sign peeling
off it in great scrolls. She makes for it gratefully, the
strange oasis, feeling like an armadillo whose armor
has been baked and buried in sand.

Carefully she brakes the carriage and peeks inside at
Carie, who is looking up lazily, back at the edge of
sleep. Someone's long lashes she'll have; they are curled
so tight they look mascaraed. Molly smiles—because
one does? Because babies drink in smiles with their
milk and grow on them? Because the smile just comes,
she sees the soft curve of chin, the eyelash shadow on
her cheeks, and wants to smile?

She doesn't want anything, only a cold drink and
sleep, or some of that acrid coffee she is breathing in;
her tight-folded life with no more shame in it but what
she cares to admit to herself, however much at a given
time, and nothing owing anyone. She, who had come
out of the divorce court like a bull into the *corrida*,
energetic, vigorous, newly discovered, unfulfilled
survivor of that dreary marriage exempted from the
need of a man to make her life around, she sits in a
clump on the hot slatted bench thinking, Wouldn't Verne
laugh? Wouldn't he enjoy the sight of it, my child,
nearly my child, here within my grasp finally, why
don't I pick her up, paralyzed, do I smile, don't I, if I
do why do I, Molly get a doll (is what he said), get
yourself a doll with detachable sexual parts for your
every mood, and a whole wardrobe of arty clothes you
can run up yourself, and spare a real child your grip,
because you grasp too tight, lady. No matter how tame
your pointy little face and your old dun hair, your fingers
on the world are not gentle. You are hungry after starving yourself too many years. Those years weren't my
fault, why should I pay you for them? Just because I
came too late, don't you bludgeon me. Your shoes
wear down in a week, your hair grows fast and crooked,
you chew up your pencils like breakfast toast, you go
around walloping pillows to get them to sit straight,
you swim like a lifeguard without stirring up the water
but you make waves in the bathtub, you look like a
mouse but you are noisy as a cat in bed and make
scratches on my shoulders and I. Cannot. Stand. It.

You looked to me like an ordinary decent woman like my own sister who was glad to have a man and live out of danger finally. I don't know what you are always nattering about. Molly thinks, crossing her legs, uncrossing them, crossing them again, looking around suddenly as though she has done some unseemly thing (she has never thought this before, not dared out loud), And you could not give me what I wanted. What does quietness have to do with ardor? Some people have to grow up secretly alive. You railed at me for every breath I took because you didn't breathe. You could never fill up the empty place in me but, dumb blind Verne with your insulted sex, what did it have to do with sex? At the end of a day you've lived together you go to bed together—that seemed plausible. But Verne was made for mounting corpses, he lived his life like a necrophile. Sex is blank, transparent, the sheets are a *tabula rasa* that you fill with your living. And I am still alive, at least for a while. . . .

She stands, looks into the carriage, feeling ruthless anger. From the carriage hood hangs a narrow gold chain that bounces back and forth like a bell-pull as she lowers her head inside to tuck the pale blanket tighter than it needs to be. She has hung it there herself, a mustard seed like a cat's eye, a slit of deep yellow for luck, her wish for Carie Lyn out of a legend neither black nor white. Once a mother whose child had died went to the wise man weeping and he told her, "Good Woman, go knock on the door of every house in the village. And where there has never been calamity in that household, never been the death of a loved one, bring from that fortunate house a mustard seed." When the woman returns to him foot-weary and defeated, overcome with the sorrows of the world, her hands (of course) empty, he tells her that she has proved once and for all that the only wisdom is to live with no love for a human and therefore no fear of pain.

When Molly hung the mustard seed from a tiny red pin stuck in the carriage roof, she had told herself, This is a fool's wish. It is Verne's dead hand, his curse of detachment. He, who else, was the wise man who counseled the noble path that is wide enough for one only; the path he is taking. But this is the mustard seed that comes from the house of joy, she had insisted to herself,. frowning to make sure the logic was on her side. This is the impossible prize.

She lifts her head from the carriage and the chain tangles in her hair. She has to cross her eyes to work the reddish strands out of the links, finally she tears a few to unhook the charm from her head. She closes the tear-shaped glass bead in her hand and holds it half-protectively, half as if to leech some of its resolution from its small folded core. She is looking idly down to the next block where dozens of wooden stoops slouch in front of matched shingled houses. They are the ones where fires obliterate whole families of ten and twelve, winter and summer. Children dodge up, down, around, dark as tree bark. Two boys near her are scrunched down right in a kind of drainage ditch eroded along the nonlawn; it is dammed with beer cans; their feet are dug into its swampy canyon sides. They must be playing hide-and-seek, the IT is counting in a singsong voice out of nowhere.

The calls blend and separate and blend again, like the sounds of civilization—she will always remember, with her whole body, she tenses right now in a kind of echo of old panic—the time, at nine or thereabouts, when she told her mother she was not staying in the summer cabin, called her a death-dealing tyrant (under her breath), rushed out slamming the screen door, and lost herself, desperately, in the real woods. She had been crying silently for half an hour, her legs scratched and bitten to the knee, cold evening air rising from the ground in waves, no trail, no light of any clearing over the treetops. She still dreaded going home to the quiet that lay over the summer, muffling every noise. But she had prayed to her imaginary best friend Veronica, who was half-magic, half-girl, and had never had parents—and had spun around to pick a direction, stopping where she thought she divined a slight pull. Ready, if it didn't lead her anywhere, to lie down and wait to be destroyed, by ants, by bears, by wind or hunger or loneliness, she had brazened through the underbrush quivering for hate and love of the lost world, when she heard voices, this very same rising and falling under the open sky, and one high shout as they finished up the count: "Eighty-ninety-a-hundred-here-I-come-ready-or-not, anyone-around-my-base-is-IT!!!"

She had stood still, at the brink of the woods, staring at them as though she had just stepped out of a space ship. How they ran and circled, tagging someone OUT. How they touched each other violently, casually, hard.

251

(basement)

KITCHEN MONEY

There is a little Americana—blond and built sort of like a boy with tits. She wears very short skirts and nothing under her sweaters, and by his shoulders her husband must be some kind of a football player. His hair comes down to his back and ends in a page boy, and their son is called Sean. That's a name Ines has never heard before. One day the girl asks Ines if she takes children into her house, baby-sitting. Oh, I have too many kids already, I can't use no more. You do? Oh yeah. Luz and Faye, Nando, Paco, Tracy, she goes on. The girl is trying to get a job as a model, she's skinny and white enough, like an extra-large egg. Good luck to her but what would Ines do with that little Sean, he looks like a cod. Even for money . . . I live in the commune, she says, but I'd never leave him with any of *them* all day. They're my friends but I'd never.

Next time Ines sees her the girl is leaning against her tree while the baby plays by the curb. She's throwing oysters into her mouth out of a little bag. She says they're oysters, raw. The bag is oily at the bottom and it's making a little stain on her chartreuse sweater. She must feel the stain sticking to her ribs. Ines goes close to her and, smiling, says she can get coats, suits, a whole line of men's clothes—36, 38, 40—very cheap. She sells it for extra kitchen money, she murmurs, shrugging. Where do you get it? the kid wants to know. Ines digs a red shoe into the grass where the runty tree's attached, and stops when she sees she's scuffing the tip.

There isn't really any silence because rush hour is going by and every car that gets to the metal plate that covers a pothole, their left tire makes a jolt that sounds like someone swallowing hard, and then a metal clunk like throwing a pot lid. A car full of kids with the radio on all the way to Canarsie takes off like the Demo Derby, tossing up pebbles.

Finally the kid says, Well, my husband never wears suits. Or coats or anything. Old shirts and—like costumes.

Costumes. What, like plays? She is thinking of Tracy as a blade of grass in the school play, Paco as Uncle Sam, keeping his finger pointed for half an hour.

I mean, you know, capes, London bobbies' caps or Salvation Army or maybe old paratroopers'—like that.

Oh. Well, I ain't got that, Ines says, moving away, apologetic. I don't get much call for any of that. She stops. He don't ever wear a suit?

The kid smiles and throws thin blond hair off her forehead. It's like long uncut grass but no color. Grass after a hot season back home. Not since I know him, she says and laughs. Beautiful teeth, like china plates. Not even for a funeral we went to one time. Some people got mad but he's, like, a believer, you know? He's got a lot of, unh, integrity, he'll never do what he doesn't want to.

As Ines moves down the block thinking about that, the kid shouts, But dresses. I'm into dresses, all kinds, wild ones—sequins, feathers and, like, shimmery old kinds of cloth? If you ever get any. Size 6.

Six, Ines says with no intention of remembering it. What is she, a little boy? Six. No sale.

259

(upper duplex)

WHY I QUIT THE GOWANUS LIBERATION FRONT

AND AT THE SAME TIME LEFT MY WIFE AND KIDS AND FLUNG MY WHOLE LIFE IN A CARDBOARD SUITCASE WHICH, IF I EVER PUT IT DOWN IN THE RAIN, WILL DISINTEGRATE AND LEAVE ME WITH APPROXIMATELY NOTHING, GIVE OR TAKE A COUPLE OF SUBWAY TOKENS:

Because on the morning of the George Street Fair, or the George Street Street Fair, or whatever the hell it was, I woke up with a headache that said, Take nothing for granted. There are two kinds of people, my old friend Henry James once told me—those who take things hard and those who take them easy. You know. Beware hot dog venders who give the wrong change and neighbor ladies who work for *Time* magazine and want your signature. Go back to sleep is what I also said, but I was supposed to help erect a giant spider between Fontaine's and Rosenberg's opposed—oh how opposed—houses, and so I swung out of the choppy surf of those sheets and summer blankets and began the morning.

I went downstairs. What is this? I asked my wife, aflap in her red and pink kimono giving Tang to my children, who, male and liberated female, aspire to be astronauts.

What is what? she answered. The twenty-third of July? Saturday morning? A hot day even before the sun came up? The Borough of Brooklyn? Kix and Cheerios? What is *what?*

I don't like her to talk that way to me, it truly cuts me. But she is a sassy girl, I assure myself, the way you like her. She makes some worth-while trouble for you, pal. And is nearly black, just barely inescapably black and vivid and has given me these two maybe black and vivid children here, Sebastian and Nineveh.

Vivid they are indeed, now that I recall, and that was the beginning of this headache I'm holding in my hands: This very Sebastian appearing in our doorway at about two this morning when I was quite involved with his mother in ways not enhanced by conversation with a six-year-old. Can I get in between you, he asked with an innocence that knocked the breathless breath out of me (for we were fortunately and purely by chance modestly under a sheet in the street-lamp brightness of that room). But just to check I asked, Why do you want to get in between us, sport? All of a goddamn sudden?

And it was the usual sort of answer—either it was sharks or skates or sting rays, or something in that category of exotic predator that sounds like a sports car but is really an invading army in a technicolor nightmare perhaps the result of a wet bed, or then again brought on, poor child, by our indiscreet though wholly legal languors down the hall.

No you may not, I told him. Go back to your own bed where a big boy belongs. I was, mind you, disappearing fast from the warm clutches of his mother's invisible possession.

She gave a lurch and I was on my own. No, don't you say such a thing. Come on in here, honey. She rearranged herself cozily as though she was on the Flatbush Avenue bus and somebody wanted to sit down next to her with a lapful of packages. She does not believe you can ask a child to get back into a bed where a nightmare's been, even if he's well awake of it. But she is a thoughtful mother, soft, the way you like her. I told myself. So Sebastian leaped over me, putting his foot precisely down on the part of me already most affronted and bereft, and slid like an ermine, long and elastic, right between the fading warmth of the two of us. I considered a hundred inadequate revenges and had to settle—such was our arrangement there, utilizing the king-size bed as it was not, believe me, intended—I had to settle for a quick but earnest pinch of anger aimed at my wife's near nipple, so recently, fervidly hardened to my fingers; and of course missed, as she turned her back to us both, and delivered an unfond tweak to the meaningless goose flesh just under her armpit.

Now what is this? I repeated to Clarette—the winy name she walks through her sober life graced by. Weren't you supposed to be down at recycling at eight-thirty to set up?

Oh that. A wave of the hand. How can I blame her for not hurrying to begin a day to be spent in a booth under a huge poster, big as a billboard, that features a *trompe l'oeil* painting of one giant-assed soda bottle with a green tree blooming inside where, in the good old days, model ships used to lie captured—and the tremendous and portentous words all around the bottle: THIS (what?) HAS BEEN RECYCLED!!! They are actually going to tote along to their booth, these believers, these naïfs of the nonreturnable generation, bins full of green and brown bottles, lovingly sorted, and enough bound newspapers and smashed tin cans for another war drive. To demonstrate what I'm not certain: But if the craftsmen can show their crafts and the artists their art, I guess these noble collectors have an unalienable right to make the most of their garbage. Poor Clarette. I'm in sympathy with anyone who doesn't get out of her kimono by nine just to help them pile it higher.

I, on the other hand, am hurrying. I argued for a rat as the proper emblem of our beloved neighborhood, or at very least a roach, or coupling roaches rampant, to signify endless and reliable proliferation. But it is the spider who won on the grounds of his picturesqueness, his ready identifiability and, not least, a leftover black widow, or whatever the damn thing was, from a block party on West Seventy-third Street last year. We were assured no one from George Street could possibly have been on West Seventy-third Street on that day; they probably checked it out door to door with signatures on one of the those clipboards.

I was not talking to Sebastian after last night but he didn't notice, glass raised, his other-worldly Tang quaffed in the gay style of an officer lifting a stein in

The Student Prince. Two weeks of silence and he
wouldn't notice as long as you didn't block his view of
the tube. Nineveh was painting her nails green. She
would soon, she informed me solemnly, be painting
her cheeks to match, alternating the green stripes with
pink, to look like Minnie Mouse. She thinks I don't
know anything, of course, but I do know a couple of
insignificant items, and a fairly good grasp of Minnie
Mouse's physiognomy is among them. But I don't really
know what her generation is into viz à viz the Ducks
and the Mice; for all I know Minnie's into orange
sunshine or purple snowflakes or harder stuff and has
suffered genetic damage. Far be it from me to intrude
my advice, so I finished my coffee, warned them, like
a drill sergeant, to keep it moving, all of it, especially
their mother's, and left. There was an air of excitement
that made me walk on the balls of my feet, like the first
day of school or an air raid. Maybe when the circus
rolls into town you feel like this, but I was born in the
city, East Ninety-fourth Street, so we only knew the
season by the big ads in the Sunday *Times*, which my
parents always answered with checks.

Fontaine was out there standing in the middle of the
deserted street. There was one bastard who hadn't
obeyed the urgent signs we had posted on the trees last
night: he'd parked his frigging little Triumph right there,
business as usual, in the middle of the block just about
where the cuchifrito booth was supposed to go. I want
to bust his windows out! Fontaine shouted, that earnest
little chipmunk face all gnarled up. Who he think he
is, he see the signs, by order of police, how big we got
to make them? He spat accurately on the dusty fender
and a thick tear washed its way down, showing blue
underneath.

The others, coming slowly out of their shuttered
houses, tucking in shirttails or straightening essentially
unstraightenable Mexican shirts and Pakistani caftans,
gathered around. Molly had her baby on her back. Mrs.
Olsen was coming at a run. They had suggestions.
Release the handbrake, roll it onto the next block and
let them deal with it. Festoon it with streamers and
pretend it's a decoration. I suggested we raffle it off.
A couple of kids volunteered to kick it to pieces. We

were still standing around, just about ready to see if Mrs. Santiago could get it to levitate, when this kid comes striding up out of the basement where what's his name lives, the kid who does the rug shampoo demos at McCrory's, and without a word—not one word, of apology, of good morning, of screw you, folks—he got in, turned on the ignition, and swooshed the thing the hell out of our way with a thunder of hoofbeats, I swear, shouting Hiyo Silver, and left us our pristine curb with only the natural shit of the day huddled in it like flowers crawling back into their chinks, and we could then begin to set up the Great George Street Follies in dead earnest and not without a few first-class second thoughts.

Now let me backtrack for a necessary instant. How did this great day, this jollity of neighbors, this togetherness so unreal and off center it will surely attract the attention of the New York *Times*, ever manage to come about? That Chico Pacheco there, public spirited though he may secretly be, with his name like a dance, is working assiduously with hard-frowning Howard Peet in his approved-pattern sport shirt open exactly to the correct half-inch under his solid-state transistorized adam's apple? (They are putting up a stage that says THE WHEEZLES AND SNEEZLES PUPPET PLAYERS.) That Doree Rosenberg, whose cunning little face this morning reminds me of nothing so much as an olive that's sat in a martini overnight, or maybe a pickled mushroom except, if you can except it, that it's the high pink Revlon must call Kindled Spirits or Effort and Enthusiasm, is tacking up on an endless pegboard the *manifestaciones folklorísticas* of her neighbors, which range from some rather terrifying photographs of noodles and—dog food is it, with all those gaping pores?—to the drawings for some medical textbook of the billion channels and locks of the Isles of Langerhans and the pink pleura of what I would take to be the left lung.

How it came about was neither simple nor inevitable but it has its own kind of semifated, i.e., half-assed, probability to it. We got one of those bonuses in the mailbox one day; long after the mail had come, some noble volunteer spirit had actually attempted to find

the appropriate orifice on these houses into which to
thrust a mimeographed page that announced its democratic intentions by saying MIRA! and then Attention!
across the top in that carefully premeditated order. The
problem, you must understand, in a "semirenovated"
neighborhood is that, after having failed to determine
how many souls, drunk or sober, still dwell behind
those out-of-order doorbells in the rooming houses where
the mailboxes have few names, let alone current ones,
then you have to decide just exactly what, on the blue
or gold or flayed-brick houses, is intended to be the
ingathering place for mail and New York *Times*. Is it
that little straw basket that clings to the entry gate on
leather thongs? Or the bean pot with fitted cover, or
does that hold mung-bean sprouts ripening? Or—for
the casual ones who take it as it comes—are you intended
merely to fling the mail through the chinks in the gate
onto the sodden leaves and old political and reuphol-
stery ads that thicken the puddles over the drain? Is the
entrance, in fact, in the basement or up the broad steps
beside the magnificent double doors retrieved from that
castle in Transylvania? I would rather canvass the World
Trade Center, both buildings, on foot, than deliver flyers
on George Street.

Nonetheless, somebody did it. The flyer invited all
"like-minded citizens" to come to a meeting at the
hippest house on the block to consider finding a new
alternative to the block association. Well now. That
wasn't a bad idea, I had to admit, though it isn't really
the way I like to spend my time. The Block Ass. did
generally innocuous thing with its dues: bought those
apologetic infant trees out there for the convenience of
the dogs, then threatened with prosecution the people
whose dogs aimed with deadly accuracy for their steps
or those same hypocritically offered trees; urged you
to vote, go pull the red lever for any twelve out of
thirteen of Ali Baba's thieves for the city judgeships;
lobbied against the bus that rattles down the block merely
taking people where they need to go in the—ah, ghet-
tao down they-ah. That sort of business. Turns its back
generally on the real problems, say, what's getting passed
from hand to hand to vein on the corner: things too
sullying to see. Clarette went to one of their meetings

once and, besides being ogled by a couple of up-tight assistant treasurer types whose wives keep everything in a bun with a rat in it, apparently mortified them by trying to talk about the real grown-up traffic the kids direct. You could hear them whispering to themselves if not to each other: But it's her own *people*. How can she say such scabrous things about those little children who could be her *cousins?*

So I went to this meeting. It was in the house of a writer, a cat who gets his kicks out of having six working fireplaces (half of which he had to discover under old wallboard, scraping, tearing with his fingernails like a man escaping from a high-security cellblock) and nothing but plants and pillows in his parlor. I think he's showing off his floors, which are half Peruvian mahogany and the other half Ugandan maple, or the other way around. We all sat around indirectly on the backs of those peasant wood choppers, on Peter Max poufs in all the forbidden color combinations, sort of waiting for the water pipe to get to us, as it were, and we all agreed—in our beards and boots and clean jeans and wash-and-wear work shirts—that the gentry on the block had flubbed it. True to their instincts they had protected their own little WASP-hegemony. We, ah, we were all in agreement on that. But what to do? Invite squatters to live in the vacant buildings! Start a free school in a basement! Make the parking signs bilingual! Get a giant speaker and alternate rock and Latin music on the weekends! Get St. Anselm's Mercy Hospital to do abortions! (Half the women in the room would volunteer to have one if that would help.) Push the pushers to another block! Take down the backyard fences! Have a block party whose theme will be Discover Thy Neighbor! (since you will all be untimely ripped off together).

The writer's wife in velvet knickers and a gold undershirt passed around coffee and macrobiotic petit-fours that tasted like you'd had a fever for a week; maybe even been in a coma. We agreed. We passed a joint to signify our accession to our three radical points that night. The light was dim; the fire crackled richly though it was May; we had vowed as homeowners— most of us having been pushed by the Misfortunes of

Economic Realities into borrowing down payments from our capitalist parents, who loved to see us crawl into that hateful bag—not to charge our tenants more than three hundred dollars a month. (If we could help it, letting conscience be our guide.) We had decided to have a multiethnic Street Fair complete with police barricades at both ends of the block to close it off even to the rest of George Street, thus indicating true inner-block solidarity (as opposed to intra-block, which comes later). We would find a cause to use the money for at our second meeting, when we could fight about how many people could relate to flower boxes, how many to gas lamps, or to arts and crafts for the kids, how many to free movies—Regis Debray? Looney Tunes?—shown on somebody's back wall. And we were henceforth to call ourselves—perhaps we could even be so incorporated, the lawyers would get to work on it—the Gowanus Liberation Front.

And here we were. My patience had been frayed close to its limits by the trouble we had with our spider, who sagged, who broke his right mooring and came perilously close to falling in the face-painting pots. Finally, looking like a magnified rubber practical joke from a Times Square novelty shop, we got it to dangle firmly but menacingly above us. The man with his trucks full of rides arrived and tried out his generators; they were so noisy the only thing you could do was play music with a firm beat over them. The teen-age girls with their hair to their behinds—these were the ones who went to the private schools where they learned the Joyous Useless Arts—hung their tie-dyed and batiked and bled-upon tee shirts on a line with clothespins: such magnificent homage to the potential of human organs exploding. Well, sure I was still horny thanks to my son Sebastian's nightmares, but that one blond girl with her twitchy little ass in pink short-shorts was shaking out and pinning up the exact unbelievable colors of the orgasm she's never had.

And so the people began to arrive, right in time for lunch. The pigs' ears sizzled, the cuchifritos and the eggplant Parmesan competed, hissing. Children walked around with luminescent dots on the ends of their noses, peace signs on their cheeks, and at around one-thirty a beer-powered man, wider than the ferris wheel, scooped a shy skinny Spanish lady into the crook of his arm and danced in dizzy circles with her. A dozen couples and a dozen singles began to whirl and shake, some of them the fantastic triple-jointed leapers who tip in three directions at once, looking nowhere, straight ahead. What does it feel like to tell your body GO and have it make its way for half an hour without you? Ah, I thought, standing at attention beside my booth, why can't I fly? Why are the souls of my feet all tarred and sticky with seriousness and the bones of my rib cage brittle, my whole life aged? Why was I born to work in the office of a publisher of high quality bad news, all of us buried under a silt of words, and not to fight and leap and twirl around in the streets, stealing breakfast from uncovered trash cans and thanking no one? Clarette was dancing alone down there in front of her boxed bottles, her pointy hips making arrows that said UP and DOWN and oh glory, her whole slick pelvis lighting up TILT. I almost abandoned my place and went down there and took her home.

So it was lovely till then—the troubles of the day minor, the pleasures ephemeral maybe but tangible: black and white and brown groups appeared to meld and separate and come together again, though of course everybody was hanging onto the friends they came with. A trampoline broke and somebody got his shoulder a little bent but fortunately it was a grownup, not a kid (which is probably why it broke). Naturally he told us he'd sue; we told him there was no one to sue. How could that be? This is happening, isn't it? It's real, we're here, it's not a dream, so there's got to be somebody to sue. Bug off, pal, wait till we're incorporated. When we become an Institution, a recurring, an annual, a perennial even, then we can begin our joyous life of constant litigation.

The puppet show, too cute for words, couldn't be heard above the music, so all you could see were flowers dancing and big wolves eating up chipmunks and then cleanly puking them up again: the moral of it all, I suppose, being that you'd better watch what you eat because some of the sweetest ickle things are first-rate

poison. My own kids surfaced from time to time to tell
me they'd won a quarter playing some kind of unoffi-
cial craps down in front of Luis's bodega, or a two-
mill grab bag of plastic monkeys for a dime throwing
darts. I told them to stick with the craps, it paid better.

I was stuck myself, now, manning the cake and
cookies. It was dreary but whoever had to bake all this
stuff in July had it drearier. The crowds danced up to
me and back, always in cycles, a dozen at a time or
none at all. I had a kid of around eleven or twelve
named Wilbert helping me, skinny, very dark, and
desperate to please. His shoes were shined. He told me
he lived down at the far end of the block in one of
those anonymous houses across from the hospital. (When
he told me that and I registered no recognition, I hastened
to assure him that I didn't know half the names of
anybody on our homey block; I don't think he believed
me.) We made a good team, he'd take orders and shovel
the stuff together, I'd take the money and make change.

After a long time, having handed out countless cookies
with rainbow sprinkles and cake that was losing its
frosting to the heat, he muttered something about my
not trusting him with the bread. I turned to say, What
bread, nobody baked bread. But, smartass that I was,
he meant the coin box. Well, I told him smiling, smiling, I didn't know if you'd like making change and all,
it can get a little hairy—you know.

Yeah, he knew, but he said he'd like that. It would
be good practice for school and all. He was glaring at
me; still polite but good at a kind of incipient militant
challenge under the eyebrows. I found myself wishing
my foulest wish, that my wife would sidle up with her
Afro, her gingerbread skin, her raisins-on-gingerbread
eyes. That wish alone should get me knifed in an alley,
if not in my own bedroom. I mean I would sympathize.
Furthermore, as the gods would have it, splitting their
fat and sloppy sides, the whole of my dear wife aspires
to the approximate color of the palms of her hands, the
soles of her feet. I know she sees herself being sucked
one day into her pale extremities, whoosh, all gone,
her toes and fingers swollen; then coming out of herself,
rising like a flower blooming, a butterfly emerging, a
parachute springing open, all bleached and wan and

happy. That best of all places, that sherry-brown buttocks, gone maggoty-white like a Rubens: like a loaf of processed Silver-cup rising in a plastic bowl. That day I will divorce her.

But she did not come to me now that I needed her, my *bona fides*, good dog, good wife; she could not abandon her bottles and cans, her wooing of the nifty faggot god called Mr. Clean. I was left alone to face this Wilbert, who looked ticked off at me, his hand clenched around a muffin, about to eat it, the ultimate vengeance: borrowing and bloody well not planning to replace it with a dime, goddamn it, stealing from the people. The People Unincorporated.

But then he collapsed, went abject. Forget it, man, skip it, no shit, he said, and turned to a customer. Did he see my fear? My power? Was he getting signals from a rooftop or a wrist radio, something from Muggers Central that said *Lay off, we get that ofay muhfuh later, in his sleep . . .?*

Just to show him I trusted him, then, I let a few minutes go by, sold a couple of deflated popovers and half a banana bread to that Martin and his tired wife in a silver pants suit who leans on him always, without seeming to touch him. Then I said with such casualness the kid deserved to pistol-whip me on the spot, bend me back over the daisy-paper tablecloth and knock my teeth right out my tailbone, Hey Wilbert, man, watch the booth a minute, O.K.? Just like that. Adding egregiously, TCB, baby. Literally. Do I like to dishonor myself or just my race?

Well, I didn't want to see any more of the fair, it'd been gyrating for hours just beyond my eyeballs and I felt a little queasy, so I went up my own steps and into the dark cool of the house.

Bad move. Every minute of this day had been flushing me with the unsettled feeling that I was approaching some last divide, some boundary, some wall—ultimate. Lurid. Real. I walked into the kitchen; the hum of the refrigerator greeted me at the threshold with its reminder of all the petty inefficiencies and annoyances of this overpriced pigpen. Sometimes it got so loud you had to raise your voice. It had no light, the week we moved in the bulb shattered in my hand when

I was putting in a fresh one. Three stitches. Now, when I turned I saw the very ultimate wall in front of me, the frigging emblem of this life my wife aspires to while I aspire to her as she might be if she were me: *the brick wall*, hung with geraniums and frying pans and a plastic shelf from the Pottery Barn, from which lentils and almonds peek out of portholes like stow-aways. The country wall that's a dead giveaway: worth two liberal votes (in '68, one for Gregory, one for Cleaver), a lifetime subscription to the *Voice*, a good double lock on the door, Lamaze lessons, and a TV set of inconsequential size crammed in a corner apologet-ically (on which I watch football and she watches Julia Child and the children learn their life from Scoobydoo).

I am too bored to move. No man can leave his wife and kids for reasons like these, he can only go on dreaming and dreaming that he will. Epiphanies are still for those who deserve them: who have a streak of originality left in them, obliterate good sense and bad logic and can fall down an endless rabbit hole. Talk about epiphanies: it had never occurred to me before this minute, this very second, that all the undergradu-ate-essay-style cant I scribble on my reports of rejected manuscripts every endless day of my working life is real. Means me. Epiphanies are not shop talk? Edito-rial shorthand for We'll Take It? Will *that* be my one epiphany? My beast in the jungle had me by the throat. The reasons in my life oppressed me, they were real, but I yawned. I positively gaped with the tedium of my tedium, ennui of my ennui.

I stood wishing I were murderous—*un crime passi-onel,* how I wished I could be roused to cut curse words out of my wife's grudging sides, or hang my engorged sex from the chandelier alongside the Pest-strip, the way they hang the tail and ears of the bulls who couldn't make it. Watch who you calling a bull there, baby, you a tse-tse fly, the refrigerator told me. I reached in and pulled out a plum. What a good boy. Are these the plums, the very ones, shrivelled in their skins and the skins whitish as though they'd been mari-nated a century in Milk of Magnesia, that the good Dr. Williams ate and left that note about, that makes my neck crawl for the simplicity, the bareness of the means of fucking *genius?* They are sour and mealy and Christ I really do think I want to die right now, or sleep a good long imitation. I will crawl in this refrigerator and perish like those kids who hide in deserted freezers. But this pile of the landlord's crap leaks so much you couldn't assassinate a goldfish in there. I'll strangle myself with the telephone cord, I pay enough for it. I'll drink cleaning fluid. But the voice of the medulla just goes plodding on, my refrigerator voice, advising aspirin and bed rest: You just get on with it, these things can't be hurried. Sooner or later, rely on it, you'll catch something, kid; and then you'll go out fighting and kicking.

So I poured myself a tall glass of leftover rosé that tasted exactly like the discount it was, and went downstairs and out, belching. Everybody was gathered around the middle of the block where they were auctioning off an afghan that made my hair stand on end in this particular smarmy weather. Some people had more foresight than I, or they just liked to play auction. The price was stopped for a second at twenty-four dollars, but they were going up fast, killer instincts grappling, wives beseeching husbands for permission to throttle their neighbor's bid.

The crumbs and leftovers made my table a good place to stay away from, flies dive-bombing, ants beginning to scout the turf. And of course, of course, the money was gone. The money box on its side, clean and empty as a baby's mouth, and Wilbert, my friend, my assistant, *mon frère,* has split.

Or has he? I was standing there smiling the smile of the damned, thinking, if you want to know, about Florence: a jewelry store on the Arno, near the middle, where, window-shopping for some silver to bring my mother, I met a girl once who had the tattoos of hands on her breasts. I was almost free of the First Annual George Street Miasma, tracing a finger around those fingers that were huge, that were a giant's leavings, when Wilbert came up to me looking anxious.

So we did our little dance. Where is it, pal? Where's what? You know what. Oh shit. Forgive me, O Lord with your blasted ears who haven't heard a word out of me from where I float trapped in this chaos, this egg of my life, lo these many years, but these are scenes I forbear to repeat. They are too demeaning, I get wound in the coils of words, of things as they seem, of this little kid, black till he's purple, a veritable eggplant of earnestness, who ends up crying real, or at least wet, tears, saying Frankie took it, I help you find him, he down by Anthony's but he tough, man, you be careful. He cut.

We trooped off to catch Frankie, who eluded us like a Casbah pickpocket or who, innocent, was just going his way. Foiled whichever he was, we walked back silently, shouldering our way through, to report the mess to The Writer, who was masterminding this whole exasperating Victory for Togetherness, and so I got to watch a man like me, an asshole that opens and closes to all the wrong cues. I felt, I know I look like this man, this William Buckley of the lower passions, the penultimate fool (when it is the ultimate fool who will save us). He considered Wilbert weeping, Wilbert wronged. One of these deep dark children—parents recent émigrés from the most desperate class of abused plantation serfs, ah yes. (Check it out.) With glasses, indicating, perhaps, an effort toward study, toward application, hope and desire. Upward, onward and off the welfare rolls forever. The thieving little bastard, does he even *live* on this block? Or does he come to play the show like the cat with the Whizzy Whip and the rusty junior ferris wheel? I don't know, I don't care, but his face was abused, washed with his desperation: He my friend, Frankie, he take it and say Don't rat on me, man, you be sorry.

So why are you ratting? Oh I am two-faced; helplessness is two-faced, his and mine. Or three- or four-faced if it gets the chance.

I don't want no trouble sir.

Don't call me sir.

Yes sir.

The Writer was getting impatient with us now. Did I have any idea how much was gone from the till? he wanted to know.

I had no idea. Was the money real? As real as Wilbert, who is not real?

You ever been arrested? I asked this kid whose frayed

shirt was sweated through, whose baggy pants rode his scarecrow hips at the danger point. I'd hate to see him in his underwear, the sight of my chunky Sebastian in his shining Jockey shorts afflicted me: my boy the color, the shape even, of a manila envelope stuffed with dollar bills.

He hesitated. For suspicion once, he told me. He didn't have to tell me that, goddamn it, he would not protect me from himself.

I shrugged and went home. Just left him there to himself, thinking what he would think, victory or defeat: his own business. I didn't clean up my crumby little table. Too much superego got me in this mess in the first place. Let The Writer come and call me a wash-out, all-around four-star fuckup, I was finished for the day, if not forever. Let the ants and the flies divide the spoils, invite the spider down. They are not shameful in their dealings.

So you see, that's how it happened that I walked upstairs again, this time with my face set, like a man resolved on flinging a rope over the rafters. I packed my shabbiest suitcase, a faded plaid, like a wife going home to Mama. High melodrama: tossing things out of the dresser and halfway across the room so they tumbled open in a childish mess on the bed. My own wife used and ill-married, my children pinched between my finger and her thumb, my prick the uroboros, snake with its tail in its mouth, belly to the ground, ear to the sky, let it delight itself a while since Clarette, her head in *its* own mouth, barely greets it when it comes. . . .

All my loudest shirts shouted out in the dark of the snapped-shut case; the dashiki I bought thinking it was a form of flattery; the purplish pants that shine to mock me. All my fly vines. How Wilbert would laugh, is laughing, should laugh. How he'd like to own them.

I picked up my suitcase and trucked on downstairs. I left a penciled note for Clarette and our children, who, reading above grade level, were sure to read it with her. It was hard to write. What should it be?

      'LIFE IS NOT A DREAM. CAREFUL! CARE-FUL! CAREFUL!' ?

or   'EXPECT POISON FROM STANDING
          WATER'?
Then   'I HAVE SLIPPED TOO FAR FROM THE
again,   MASK OF MY TRUE FACE, AND SO I HAVE
          LEFT THE EYEHOLES BARE'?
or   'I DREAMED THAT WE ENTERED ROME
          AS TRIUMPHANT CONQUERORS. AND I
          THOUGHT OF THE ENTRY INTO THE
          ETERNAL CITY. BUT I WAS IN THE RANKS
          OF THE BARBARIANS'?

But why confuse the poor girl more than I must
simply by being my ordinary condescending self? She
has never had a literary bent but today is the last day
in the world I would want to make her regret it. So I
wrote simply:

DEAR. AND DARLING. THERE IS NO OTHER
WOMAN. I STOLE THE MONEY. TELL
EVERYONE.

Then, an afterthought, I added the I Ching I knew I
would throw if only I had some pennies in my pocket.
But my pennies had gone for change at the cake and
cookie stand, I had cast my last little bread upon the
waters and see where it had landed me. But I knew, I
knew what it would be if I were to play it out, all six
throws, and Clarette likes the Ching. It speaks sense
to what little power we have to choose; speaks softly
to her better parts and, miraculous, doesn't mess her
hair much. I put the book in the last air space in my
suitcase.

NINE AT THE TOP MEANS:

The bird's nest burns up.
The wanderer laughs at first,
Then must needs lament and weep.
Through carelessness he loses his cow.
Misfortune.

Then added, though it came from another page:

No blame, no blame.

Just let the misfortune not be theirs, I thought, let Frankie, Freddie, whatever the strongbox artist's name was—if there was such a person in sneakers, on horse, running across the backyard fences—let him not maim my children looking for me. Let him not abuse my wife's fallow charms no matter how she receives him, with hosannahs or with police whistle. But let there *be* a Frankie, somewhere, somewhere else.

It was hopeless. I squeezed into my swollen suitcase the skinny Saturday *Times* Clarette would never miss. I put two more stone plums in my pocket that bulged now as if I had a gun, and I went downstairs on tiptoe, closed the front door gently, and snuck off down to the corner to learn how the Gowanus Liberation Front had already put up its gates—for inner-block security and a hint to the likes of me. But I don't take hints easily; omens yes, innuendoes never, nor rumors, nor compacts nor conspiracies. Painfully I scaled the gates, dropping my plaid suitcase, my bandanna on the end of a stick, down on the other side, happy there were no faces looking up at it astonished, as if it were a bomb. My only misgiving, as I went over the top myself, was that its weak seams were already beginning their slow disintegration from the shock of the fall.

262

(The Eyebrow of the Moon Family)

SALLY AND ME

A story to be told from a distance: Me and Sal, for example, holding hands. Our arms reach down to the same place exactly, so we can hold onto each other conveniently and unobtrusively, with no bent elbows. E.g., the time we were walking through A & S on a crowded Saturday. Sal was scouting for the best table to lift something from, peering into faces to catch the guilty unblinking stare (that he expected but never found) of a plainclothes shoppers' spy. The only thing about this sport that bothered me was that Sal didn't give a damn what he was putting under his jacket. I believe in copping what you need—there's a kind of deep and moral stealing that gives the finger to Mr. Abraham and Mr. Straus and all their hairless little accountants all at the same time. That gets you what you want and need on your own terms, no apologies. But it wasn't worth the chance if you didn't feel that little leap of lust for the thing as your hand closed over it: a satisfaction absolutely sexual. But Sally, Jesus, he's going to get caught sometime with a pair of toddler's sneakers in his pocket, or a set of potato skewers, or a book called *Your Diabetes and How to Live with It*. I mean—I've made this sort of convenient pact with myself and the stores—I pay for about half of what I take but I love the things I steal, I leave the clepto-business for my little passions. Sally calls me Robin Hood and steals the way he'd like to murder: because he respects nothing enough to want it.

This particular Saturday it wasn't a store detective with whose convinced gaze I locked, but my parents'. Their eyes followed mine on a single string. They looked at me without a word. My mother's taffy-green sweater was thrown loosely over her shoulders; her equivalent of rolled-up sleeves. My father had that trapped look of a man-among-men on his way to the wicker furniture department. Sal stood next to me holding my hand but that was the point of all this: our arms were at our sides like the two arms of a single person. In the shoving and backing of the crowd between the handbags and the specials tables full of clanking silverware and mod bath mats, it was not at all clear that I wasn't alone. But even so they looked at each other in a flicker fast as a snake's tongue (faster than I could look at Sal, even) and, without a word to me or to each other, they pushed on past stalled shoppers, baby strollers, clerks, toward the elevators.

I am Naomi Kriegel, and I feel like the Ancient Mariner. I am twenty-two years old and have lived all my life in Brooklyn. At the moment I am living in what I call my halfway house on George Street. There may be those who think it's a commune, the people on the block do, and they'd like to lynch the landlord but he's black so they have to be respectful. (He's found the key, you see; ever since his rooms here have fissioned—committed fission?—he finds he can make five times the rent on us, eleven of us, shoplifters and petty grifters all, with noble motives, and at the same time, would you believe it, he's made it onto the Women's Page of the *Times* for being a "friend of the hippie" who drives a Thunderbird.) But the truth is, there's nothing very deeply communal about the odd lots and broken sizes in a home (*sic*) for runaways. Everybody here calls it the Eyebrow of the Moon Family. I call it a halfway house because they're, most of the others, halfway up the stairs and halfway down, all these Christopher Robins, clutching whatever bears. For myself, though, it's more or less a literal halfway between Flatbush where I grew up, my father's garden in its way—and Brooklyn Heights, Willow Street if you please—where my mother finally dragged him the same way she yanked him up to see the wicker furniture that Saturday: she remodeled him but I stepped out before she could do me over.

My father drove a cab for twenty-six years. Before that he was what they called a "hacker" in our old neighborhood, he drove families to the Ketskills in his limousine, a.k.a. a black fender-beaten 1946 Chrysler with a high slit of a rear window, almost like a Rolls. His greatest pleasure, from what I remember, was to put his flag down, his off-duty sign on, and sit around in Garfield's, that Radio City of cafeterias, the only thing in all of Flatbush that was open twenty-four hours a day, and drink midnight tea with his friends, and eat a giant fresh bagel. They'd have the morning *News* tucked in their windbreaker pockets, and they'd sit back against a gold-flecked pillar and reflect first on the Dodgers, then on the day's earnings and the day's *tsouris,* balancing them out like columns in red and black.

Now, however, having been kicked upstairs through the ranks of the hackers' union, by whatever combination of luck and brains and connivery no one is close enough to my father to know—all those noisy-mouthed men, the Jewish Mike Quills—he is under indictment by some newfangled mayor's grand jury for ticket-fixing, inspection fudging, all manner of little diddling of his thick fingers in the till. Which only proves he's just like everyone else, my mother says; in return for which she has chargeplates at Saks and Bloomingdale's with our good WASP address on them, and goes around hoping no one will recognize his name from the papers. I personally like Daddy's thievery, though I wish he were better at it. It's our father-and-daughter act, and I see where I got my light fingers from (though ladies aren't supposed to indulge). It's my luck, though, that instead of having his gratitude for my understanding, the bastard hasn't talked to me in a year. He doesn't drive any more but if he did, all the cigar rings he used to save for me, and the Canadian dimes his fares pawned off on him—those and sixty cents the first eighth of a mile would buy me a ride around the corner in his cab.

I graduated from Abraham Lincoln High School, where I was so bored I had fantasies of putting a hand grenade in my gym locker. My mother used to tell me that boredom was a sign of talent. I learned shorthand just in case. I was a hall monitor as many hours a day as I could arrange to be out of class, so I could sit and read novels while I guarded the door to the second-floor stairs, against what I'll never know. I went to Brooklyn College for two semesters, a little less. Then, during my final exam in psychology I stood up, shoveled all my carefully laid-out ballpoints into my big bag that was crammed with crib-sheets, whispered, "Excuse me" to the girl next to me who had extended her legs like a catatonic as soon as she saw the questions, and dropped my blue books into the wastebasket at the front of the room. I know I was smiling brightly and innocently at the proctor, my professor's wife in her raincoat, who called out to me as I disappeared fast down the hall. So, unexpectedly, I left college forever. I had filled two books with my views, my teacher's views, I should say, on the subject of cognitive dissonance and the double bind. Double blind? I don't remember. Anyway: if cognitive dissonance had been a true and authentic theory, I would have been desperately happy with my college education precisely *because* it was such a thorough pain in the ass and, free or not, expensive in its way. So cognitive dissonance was demonstrable bullshit, only I wasn't allowed to say it. Catch-22.

The end of college was also, of course, the beginning of the end of mother-love, father-love, uncle- and aunt-love too. If I'd dropped out of Wellesley, say, they'd have disowned me plain and simple. Brooklyn College didn't arouse their passions quite so totally but it was still, clearly, a gesture of some sort. (My mother accused me of snobbery: would I have dared to quit Wellesley?) The big question remained the same: For this my father was courting prison? Prison? Our cold war dates from that day. Like cognitive dissonance, I suppose, all that love was true and authentic and logical only if you needed to believe it.

I am not pretty, in my eyes or in anyone else's, nor am I particularly built, as they say. Therefore, refusing to take the easy out of hanging around MacDougal Street with the other bagel babies (so they were called, those who did) till some stud, black or white, decided to do me a favor in a hallway—instead, I went with a boy in my honors math class, just before my sixteenth birthday, to what must have been the most absolute dark in the Borough of Brooklyn. He had his cousin's car and a learner's permit that didn't let him drive legally after dark within city limits, but this boy was bent on being a real sinner. So we lined up with the rest of the crowd of submarine race devotees along the bank of Sheepshead Bay off the Belt Parkway. It was so dark it was like the fun house. I had trouble remembering who it was who was threshing away above me breathing Sen-Sen in my eyes with the rhythm of an old-time locomotive, and when it was all done (for him, he too having forgotten anyone was with him) I remember sort of half dreaming as if I had dozed for a few unlikely minutes down by the bay and some sea animal had crawled up, slimy, from below the pilings, had bit me painfully between the legs, and had retreated to its secret life, invisible under the water, covered with blood like something wounded. For an initiation, I assume it was about average.

O.K. After that taste of college and all the assumptions it let others make about me, not to mention the ones I could make about myself, I began getting those jobs girls will always be able to find in New York City, even with *cum laude* degrees, at the fringes of other people's professions. I worked with four-year-olds in a dark downstairs Headstart center for six months—decided children made me better than I ordinarily could be. Then they lost their funds. I worked for a doctor who was doing research but quit when the ultimatum was clear—his Girl Fridays hung around after five Tuesdays and Thursdays and performed a few tasks the lady at the employment agency never mentioned, let alone gave me a speed test in. Then, more of the same: financial aid office of a university, waitress at an intolerable singles place called The Scene of the Crime, where I had to wear something that felt like somebody else's bikini. God. That was the year I was nauseous every morning when I woke up; I'd have preferred morning sickness.

But my friends, the ones I used to play trading cards and jacks with, whose lipstick and gym suits and homework I borrowed—their solutions were worse than the problem. Marriage to junior-high gym teachers, and their equivalents. (Success is a guidance counselor or fourth assistant principal.) Marriage to boys going into their fathers' business. (Failure is a boy going into *your* father's business.) College for as long as it took to achieve "betrothal" in the *Daily News*. (The *Times* was for "climbers.") They all took swimming for their gym requirement so they could bathe their diamond rings in the pool.

My best friend managed to get to Bennington somehow: she had a histrionic bent and played the part of a destined Bennington girl at her admissions interview, to which she went shrouded, like a new widow, in layers of black. The day she received her acceptance letter she changed her name from Sima to Siam. I did admire her for guts and talent uncommon on our block but I could hardly have emulated her. I consider myself sane and sturdy and that will have to do, goddamn it. I remember to take salt along to the picnic, while Sima is busy forgetting the hard-boiled eggs. She, in spite of all her bread-kneading and batiking, has nails out to there; they have occasionally spent a season green or purple or swirled with rainbow lacquer. I bite mine. It's a good thing she's not my sister.

Or put it this way. When I was fourteen I called my red-brown hair "fox-colored." But I have grown into it. I have a frecklish skin that I wouldn't want to touch— it looks like the underside of something, though I'll never strain to figure out what. My nose even my mother calls "generous." If I were really to live on Willow Street with my parents, the neighbors would have me there on sufferance: basically, like my father's, it is not a Willow Street face.

So. I have been piling all my modest discoveries high against the inside of my skin and bone, like a levee, sand-bagged with serviceable insights. That's my education. I was afraid, sometimes, that they would make me invulnerable and entirely too self-sufficient, but there are no alternatives, are there, besides willful stupidity? Perspective is probably the worst thing a girl can have—when you have perspective your hips don't wobble when you cross the street and you keep your legs well shut of the cocksmen you meet every hour on the hour or not at all (though it all comes to the same). But it was all right. That all washed away in the flood of Sally Amado's revenge.

Prospect Park. Someone with me knew someone with him. He glinted like a knife. I was already writing my weekly letter to Sima. (You know what a loyal friend I'd have to be: me writing her letters saying "Don't get involved with him, Sim—you'll regret it," she writing back, eventually, to tell me he's back with his dumb little apple-pie wife but the abortion went fine and she may, just only *may,* be pregnant again, kid.)

Oh the clichés! If Sima had said what I felt . . . how he looked like some animal, sleek and caged. But it was all slipping away, I was moving away from firm ground like a boat inching away from the rotten wooden pilings, smoothly, irrevocably. (I see now the difference between Sima and me, though: she makes that journey out and back like a ferryboat. Better call me the *Titanic.*) But it was like some damn *Ladies' Home Journal* story—things actually can sink in your chest, your stomach. They also did something—no words for it and the magazines you pick up at the checkout counter of the supermarket never mention it—some covetous grasping movement just where I wanted to have him, inside, where I was empty all the time, all the time no matter who was irrelevantly in me for a few sad stupid minutes once in a while when there didn't seem to be any other way to get rid of him.

We started walking, a little stunned for talk. At least I was. It was Eeyore's birthday. Grown men and women dressed up like Eeyore and Piglet, Winnie and Heffalump, carrying canvas banners. Moist-eyed parents pushed strollers full of sheepdog-haired children forward to see the procession of furred animals as though an important politician were going by; the kids in their extraordinary-colored corduroys, cadmium yellow, burnt sienna, royal purple, straight, uncut, from the tube.

Now I have to remind you, here, that I did not grow up with the likes of Christopher Robin and Winnie the Pooh; that kind of thing, insofar as he and my mother knew about it, was considered pantywaist stuff by my father—faggoty English kids who talked fancy nursery-English. I ran into them during my stint at Headstart—pretty fancy for those kids too, but possible; not impossible—and now in my job at the library. So when Sal asked what in the hell was going on I was able to answer. But I couldn't explain. I said, meaning it, "You'd like Eeyore, actually. No, you'd like Winnie— he's the Bear of Little Brain . . ." I gave up. But even that much was a foot in the door for Sal's worst fears of what I was underneath. He's never forgiven or forgotten it, in our worst arguments I'm suddenly turned into a rich WASP with a nanny, giving up high tea to have a beer with my funny little spic. What my mother wishes for her grandchildren. I wish, that day, we'd walked in the other direction.

We did, eventually. He took me down to see his friends, the park people. We walked down past the Frisbee players, the noisy kids fumbling baseballs, the thump of the soccer players in their shorts falling on the ball, to where the green benches began. A few of his friends—so-called, whether he knew them or not— were flying, zooming behind their eyes. They weren't Black, most of them, they weren't Puerto Rican, they looked to me to be the Irish and Italian and Jewish children of Bay Ridge and Park Slope a half, a quarter of a generation younger than we were, the lumpen-children whose parents used to know where they were. There were two girls in bell-bottoms, true Flatbush, swaying and singing off key together, like my unfunded four-year-olds. No, like banshees, or lifers lost on a back ward. I didn't—how many people do?—know what it was like to be a bell swinging, ringing out joyously and then buckling with the pounding of the clapper again and again till your brains would rattle. I thought they were having fun. A little song for Eeyore's day? The girls split, suddenly, and ran up the asphalt path that led to the triumphal arch at Grand Army Plaza. Out there where the naked granite soldiers writhe in sexual battle, locked in the middle of traffic. Maybe the girls walked right out across all ten lanes of bellowing cars and sat down under the statue to cool off. Or jumped in the fountain and sank.

Sal told me quietly that of the twelve or fifteen people we could see from where we were standing on the path, maybe two or three would be dead next year by Eeyore's birthday. He was exactly my height; I thought it was remarkable that I could look straight into someone's eyes, as though that gave me an advantage, would get me way into the back of them, deep, deep in; a headstart.

"I might be dead too," he said, and looked away toward a red kite rising on the horizon. It was wonderfully melodramatic but I let myself be impressed. "You'd get pretty good odds," he added, and smiled, and so I didn't believe him.

I was working in the library then. My hours were flexible. A couple of times I'd reach across his brown back and call them at work and tell them I was having back trouble. I'd change shifts. Then we'd stay there on the floor on our air mattress all morning. Broad daylight poured in on us. I wrote him a poem once and left it for him when I went to work.

he is short but ends in long fingers
he is whittled to a point
concentrating he is a knot in wood
carrot in a furrow
    (i am the furrow)
and all our fine hairs dance

He was out with his friends when I came home but I had my answer, scrawled in his ten-year-old's handwriting on the back.

No   I say shit to all that
No carrot   no wood
I am an angry Spic
with a capital S
who eat no shit
with a small s
and this girl Naomi
who love me and is hungry
gots a lot to learn!

The thing about Sal is that he will not be deceived, except by his own conning and then only till he can catch himself, spin himself around. Look at it this way: Say the mayor comes and puts his hand on Sally's low shoulder that's bony as a hanger. Sal shrugs it off impatiently, turns and says, "You think you got a hand anybody'd be glad to have—delighted to have—resting on him, man. What's it like to have a hand everybody wants, all the girls cream over it, grown men want to get patted like puppy dogs? You ever just hold that hand up, a piece of flesh, it's divided up five ways just like everybody's, and give it a little thought? I mean, inside?"

Or the President says, "Mr. Amado, I see you are a member of the Respected Delegation of Upwardly Mobile Inwardly Hostile and Outwardly Docile Puerto Rican Under-Achievers, Inc., is that correct, sir? Tell me if I'm wrong." To which Sally answers, "Shit, sir, honky, sir. Gimme five."

Sal is going to be a writer, he says proudly and with a sheepish downward thrust of his head, both—the only reason I believe he is serious, because only the things he means most desperately are worthy of that double glance, inward and outward. So he has an even better phantasy: since my parents have moved to Willow Street they have a new neighbor: Norman Mailer lives, sometimes, on Willow Street. Sally wants to go knock on his door.

"You can't."

"Why not? He's a neighbor."

"Well. I don't know him. I don't even *live* there." He reduces me to statements of stunning stupidity. "Anyway he lives way up on the next block. And I wouldn't know him if he lived next door."

"Ah, 'know.' 'Know.' What, like in the Bible? Come on." He smiles his very unlikely healthy white smile. "Come on, I'll bring him some stuff to read. He'll want to meet me, shake my hand. 'Hey, spic, pretty nice.' Hit me on the arm, dance around a little, feint, jab." He boxes with the air.

"Well, you go without me, O.K.?" What I'm thinking is, getting a little confident there, Amado? A little

Populist conceit? He idolizes the not-so-new writers
who have dug themselves out of the debris of their
working-class childhoods (though his own was unem-
ployed-class, a difference). He writes love letters to
Pete Hamill and Jimmy Breslin, reads me Joe Flaherty
with dramatic gusto as though the words were his.
"Impious bastards!" With his dictionary, for words
like "impious." "But where are *we?*" and he hits
himself in the chest. "Where? Show me. The whole
Voice is Irish, what isn't Jewish went to St. Francis
Xavier. Where's one Spanish name? Jose Torres?" He
spits.

Well, I like all that. I'd rather see him learning from
his dictionary than taking those psych exams that
finished my head and made me prejudiced about a lot
of things. There are only two problems for Sally. Neither
of them is innate or necessary, I tell him, but he doesn't
appreciate the optimism and he has to look up "innate."

One is a childhood he will not talk about; instead is
going to write about (if he ever stops writing letters to
those who are writing about *their* childhoods). He claims
it's that childhood that doesn't let him. That he never
learned to sit still. And conditions are never quite right,
he doesn't have a place to concentrate, a chair, a wall,
the wind is blowing from the wrong direction, the
moon's on the wane, it smells like the city's about to
burn up, something is leaking from the manholes, I
don't know. It's those times that I suddenly see a thousand Sallys in their little rooms all over the city, invent-
ing new reasons for each morning's failure. All they
do is write on walls. "Sal A. as Norman/LAMF!"
"Blessed is the Fruit of Thy Loom. Jesus!" Well, he
tells me, you go be a critic then, it's a hell of a lot
easier. I cook the food, you say it needs more salt, tell
me who worked harder? It's not a contest, I tell him.
Who says? he answers.

The other little problem, may all his off-duty saints
forgive me, is the one he told me about that first day in
the park, but so dramatically that I didn't believe him.
That after he's written the Great Puerto Rican Novel,
he's got to live long enough to get uptown with it.
Jesus, this is why it's all going to end, and I'm going
to put my eyes out or something so I can see blankness

straight ahead. I don't want to see Sally dead.

"You want to go meet Gloria Steinem high on bennies? Why don't you go do something in the streets instead of sitting here stoned punching your fist with your palm?"

His contingency plans are all for doing something. What they are contingent upon he has never told me but that's a word he likes. ("You sound like my goddamn wife." It has been five months: the first months gentle, all this aimed at something, I tell myself, pleading, besides me . . .)

C.P. #1: Placing bombs in unlikely places. Infiltrating a political group (he knows nothing about politics, only about anger, which is not the same). "That liberal crap, you been watching the six-o'clock news again, no wonder all you can do is vote for those faggots every year." He can't name a single bunch worth double-crossing and the only bombing he really wants to do is in his own head. One day when I was pleading with him to go join the Young Lords and get an education (a sure way to put myself out on the street but better than this slow bleed) it occurred to me, one of those real flashes like pain, that he pretended all this politics for me. He wanted to make his failure fashionable for me.

C.P. #2: Testing half a dozen forms of suicide, like Russian roulette, to see what it feels like to die. Almost die. Without caring. He's gotten into the Camus on my bottom shelf. "Almost die? I thought you were already doing that." "Naomi, you're a turd," he says levelly. "You're a goddamn patriotic middle-class whore. You put out for the Marines."

I won't ask him why everything gets back to sex in the end: at the beginning maybe. Sex is only, like, the medium in which he suspends his venom. But I won't ask because I've had mine, finally, and I can't fly in the face of it. Any minute, though, he's going to try to end his argument by placing my hand on his fly to feel how he gets as soon as we raise our voices. Like Pavlov's dogs. I call that a perversion. "My mamí and her man Raoul always did it after they cut each other up. You like that?" His knife eyes, razor eyes, saying, "*Puta*, don't think you're any better than that."

Instead he shakes an envelope, takes something orange, with two yellows, washes them down with warm beer, and then looks at me a long time. There's a lot of white in his eyes.

"Sally," I tell him, "you are not basically a serious person."

He glares. "I'm getting sick of this."

"If you're looking for something to *do*, why don't you go back and finish high school?"

He has begun to play around the rim of a bongo drum he keeps in the corner, some drum with an Indian name. Something that won't hit back.

"You ever hear your mother coming out of your mouth?" He jabs the center of the drumhead. "Your classy lacquer-haired mama?"

"Why is it always *class* standing there between us? Or color. Is that all there is?" I have to raise my voice. He goes on playing, louder, slamming his palms down, slapping the drum skin. I can feel him pummeling my ass, my cheeks tighten with every smack.

"Class now! I thought it was sex that's 'always between us, Sally baby.' You got to make it all one thing, right, get us all shoveled in some bag tied up nice and neat."

I have begun gathering dirty glasses and ashtrays full of what looks like mouse droppings.

"But class, yeah, that'll do for today. Right, teacher, check. You're slumming and I'm climbing. The great Americano ideal. You need a sex manual, you look it up in the Constitution. Hear ye, hear ye: All people are created equal screwing and getting screwed. Screwsville."

He is jabbing so hard he hits his own hand, then shakes it in pain.

"For Christsake stop that, you're not in the jungle." I'm supposed to cower. His eyes are getting sharp and maybe they're terrified at bottom too, maybe not. But they're sleek with a water that only his pills can dredge from him. He never cries that way for me.

But he's right. There's a bottomless chasm between us because what he's saying, way down, is that even though I'm heading out to find a warm sane bed for the night where the only sound I hear will be the grind-

ing rise and then the free-falling of some horny boy—
I do that now for a rest from him, sometimes—he's
right, he's right. I've got myself to keep hold of. If I
lose myself tonight I can find myself in the morning. I
can say I deserve better. He exudes self-disgust thick
as the smell of a slept-in undershirt. I take two simple-
minded Excedrin before I go. Do they have a number
for this particular headache?

I slam the door and go soundlessly down the hall.
Where to, where to? All our friends are his. I want to
go somewhere where I'll be thanked, where someone
doesn't even know my name. Hector down the block
tries to cop a feel—that pathetic old-time junior high
school sport—every time I go by. The good-looking
one who sits on the front steps down there waiting for
all the women in the world to just go pouring by. But I
know he'd talk a lot, he'd think he had to whisper and
woo and try to play Romeo in his best West Indian
loll. I'm not up to it. Go stand around with the hookers
on Fourth Avenue. Whose voice is that? Sally's? My
mother's? My own.

Well, way down, 270 or so, near the corner, there's
a strange guy, very good-looking in a pallid way, who
sells rug shampoo up at the five-and-ten. I assume he's
an actor out of work because he has this incredible
delivery: "If you *don't* know how to *do* it, let me *show*
you how to *do* it!" with a little hip-twitch that makes
rug shampooing the farthest thing from your mind.
One time I complimented him on his style and I began
to see it was *his* style. In the time it took to walk from
Livingston Street to George I think I was proposi-
tioned. That is, he sort of hinted to me about sharing
the leftovers. I start off in that direction. So: Sal has
freed me so I can dish myself out to the hungry like
hot soup. An achievement to be proud of.

His orange sunshine, his purple furies. Later, when
he's made it, if he ever gets his bad dreams down on
paper, and he's driving his Maserati back to park it on
Baltic Street over near Red Hook, on his mother's
dusty-shingled block—then he can fade again, in and
out, and it'll be a different, more respectable kind of
cop-out: when you're famous, when *Esquire* puts you
on one of their "In" charts, then it's debauchery.

Dissipation—well, you assume there's got to be something there to dissipate. A fall from heights. Tragedy, not melodrama any more: to be mourned by strangers! The perils of the rich and the beautiful. Now he's a common P.R. head with talent, dreams and the kind of charm that's so ineffable I can't remember what it is when I'm this angry. When you're Salvador Amado from Red Hook, last of six, built about as thick as the punk you light fire crackers with, burning at one end, making all that color and empty noise—pop-pop— you're a dumb kid high, low, never level, goofballs, cocaine, speed, uppers, downers, murderers, and one of these days when I find a bent spoon on you, you will have chosen, Sal. You'll be a dumb loser whose girl, wet eyes or no, has split.

The rug-shampoo man is home, alone. His basement is barren. He doesn't say a word. No hypocrisy anyway. Closes an open shutter, turns me around twice, smiling, turns on all the lights, slowly takes all my clothes off, murmuring, then all his clothes off. With his back turned he is very strange, like some graceful pale jungle animal about to take off through the woods on wobbly legs. I am enjoying the look of his peculiar transparency—after Sal and all his dark assertion— when I suddenly realize, seeing his thin shoulders jerk, his cottony hips leap and then collapse as though they are suddenly hollow, that he has come in his own pale hand. I stand there stone naked, ready, befouled by my own inane desperation (let me not call it lust). Then he begins to laugh, with shame I suppose. "I don't know, I don't know," he is saying as he tries to find something to do with the mess. "Don't be offended, dear. It's your friend, the little dark one—" He has found a hanky, with which he swabs everything in sight.

And I am thinking somebody ought to drop a bomb on all of us and have done once and for all.

Another couple of months. Uphill? Downhill? Only in the movies do people get on chutes and plummet or leap in one direction at a time. Months together give you time for all kinds of scenes:

We went down the steps holding hands, our coats flying in spite of the cold. "Wait, lemme get some cigarettes.''

So I came into the dark of Luis's bodega while he picked the money I've given him, penny by penny, out of his tight pants pocket. The air changes at the threshold of this place, not warm but sour: these ancient cheeses turning to stone, to perfect pitted marble, the stale cod beached on a sack of rice, everything gritty with dust and depression. Nothing moves in here. Maybe we needed a candle, Sally and me; if he wouldn't get mad, insulted, I'd get us one: PEACEFUL HOME, maybe. Or WORK CANDLE, that and a hot foot might get him going. If they worked, though, Luis wouldn't be in such trouble himself. I hate this place, I never go near it when I'm alone. It is plague-ridden, I can almost see the X on the dust-mottled glass door. There must be rats waiting down in the cellar. But Sal feels comfortable here, the A & P gives him goose bumps. Sometimes Sal mutters about the way I feel. "I thought places like this are exotic to people like you. You ought to be so honest about me—deep down this place is a stink to you, it's different, no matzoh balls, he don't sell halvah.''

"Yeah, look at her, Luis," I heard him saying, and he turned indulgently to me and then whispered a little to Luis, that little dark man with the shy mustache. Luis guffawed, half real, his eyes absolutely disappear into his forehead, it's some *macho* extravagance, but half fake, obliging, desperate. Sally wriggled his hips, rolled them, raunchy, talked faster Spanish than a disk jockey, and they collapsed again, heads together. The way I dance? The way I screw? Then he looked at me next to the bread rack ruffling the sleepy cat, and waved an arm. "But—" he said, so this was for me "—but then, see, she go and put a time clock in next to the john so I got to punch in when I take my first piss in the morning!''

Luis was hooting. Enough of that and all his careful can castles will fall down around him. They can laugh in Spanish too, you know. It's a different kind of laugh altogether, comes from the gut, phlegmy and rolling, and they echo each other. I went outside and waited, standing next to the bare chained-up tree. These trees never look like the babies they are; they just look like they're dying. Still, I leaned one numb arm against the cold elephant-skin bark and it supported me and my anger. Supported and supported and supported me.

Sal took me home to Baltic Street, closer to the river, one day at three o'clock to see what he came home from school to all his life, the unmade beds and spare shaggy mattresses, the oleo puddle on the kitchen oilcloth. (It looks to me like he's tried to go on living in the same kind of house. But I didn't suggest it.) His mother in her muddle, missing the farms of the Island, he said. ("The farms?" "The farms.") She was off doing piecework in a handbag factory, scabbing. "You know what's politics for my mother?" he asked me in the closet dark of the hall. "How many kids you got in your bedroom when you're screwing. That's it—rich men make noise, poor men put their pillow in their mouth so they don't wake up the house 'cause the house is all in there with them."

Sal, Sal, Sal. The word means salt? It should if it doesn't. Wounds rubbed hard with sweat, tears, sperm, blood, till they vibrate with pain, I can see the waves rising off him like heat-warp off a road. He showed me a picture, lifted it off the television gently: all or most of his brothers and sisters are clustered under him like a class picture. On his tough little nut-face there is a look that says, "I'm the one that bites." He has one arm raised in a salute or a windup or the first stage of a wallop in the direction of the cameraman's bent head. What does he have in his hand? His other fist is buckled to his chest in self-defense; it proves he's about to deserve trouble. He had been kicked out of public school, then Catholic school, for unnumbered offenses before he was eleven. (Hadn't my mother told me boredom was a side effect of talent?) Would the nuns believe him if they saw his eyes flitting—badly trained for speed but speeding anyway—over the bestseller list, the fiction reviews, the history? They would say all anybody ever says, watch out, it's a con. Sally Amado is a thief and everything he says is stolen goods.

But he taught me Johnny-on-a-pony and skelly. I took him to the country on the bus and we picnicked and did all those slow motion bits they do in bad arty

movies when people are supposed to be falling in love.
I could feel it, even my hair turned back to fox-colored
and rose and fell slowly on my shoulders as I ran through
goldenrod. But he was allergic to hay and God knows
how many other green things out there and, laughing,
we had a good talk about how your mind alone can
make welts rise between your shoulder blades. He was
like kids I knew in junior high who threw up when they
ate non-kosher meat: he was supposed to thrive on
concrete, so he must have thought Liberty, New York,
was a betrayal of his blood.

"What about those farms?" I asked.

"I don't know," he answered soberly. "Too late, I
guess. It's even too late now for my Mamí."

At the same time we were looking over each other's
shoulders into the past, like an alcoholic he spent half
his time slightly out of his head, and the next whole
day apologizing. He and his rainbow of friends and
their rainbows of junk. Their rituals of sniffing, their
matter-of-fact guzzling, as though they had a little bottle
of aspirin and a big headache. If he had a chance at a
job—if it came begging, I mean, since *he'd* never go
begging—I could rely on it: he'd be coming up out of
some unholy "mistake"—you don't take green bananas
with pink snowflakes, you never mix black holidays
with white memories, yellow, gold, fuchsia. I've
suppressed most of it, and I've suppressed his friends
as well, none of them fit to be his friends except that
they had all those colored favors to exchange. I am a
Puritan about it now, if I never was before. Those
benign-looking little capsules will never touch me, they
are like rapists, but you can only see that—here we go
again—if you want to. Sally's ace was to assure me
that if it weren't for him I'd be deep into the stuff
myself. He said it was like keeping a clean house: it
gave me something to use against him, so I could
remind him all the time what a worthless slob he really
was. Look, I would say, look how they seize control of
you! You're not a worthless slob, *that's* the point! I
told Sally he was a secret queer, or worse, and didn't
even know it, maybe that was what the rug-shampoo
man knew—I mean, he likes to be ridden, flailed,

spread-eagled, flattened, cowed, ordered to jump, to bend over, to suck his own unwiped tail or anybody else's—all for an hour's vacation from himself.

When I told him that, he just said, "You learn that in your psychology class while you was still paying attention?"

I smiled at him, it was all I could do, but bitterly. Then he hit me so hard, right on my nose, that it bled and bled, all over my bare chest. It looked like someone had sliced me in two. I let it bleed until I could reach in and pull out my heart.

I am walking down George Street fast, across the cobbles of Leon, going as if I have someplace to go. I feel like myself, choked on tears, my daily bread, only a little more vivid: the clarity of an upper and the sadness of a downer.

Then I realize I'm going home. Around and down Atlantic Avenue toward the river. The sun has long since fallen in, behind a big ship that's parked at the flute end of the avenue. The sidewalk's so lumpy it may truly be the crust of the earth. There's dirt down there somewhere, it's not just in cemeteries. Earthworms? Salamanders? Not in South Brooklyn? In Brooklyn Heights, there are, there's life in the yards and window boxes, by order of the Landmark Preservation Society. Every worm a landmark, indestructible.

It's a long walk. I climb the wide granite steps of the old house, the authentic grandfather to our heap on George Street that was built later for a different class entirely, for the copiers. Wide as a brood hen under those sooty brick hackles: my mother's dream, Washington Square, the kind of house Henry James had in mind.

Does the prodigal daughter, returning on the run, knock, ring, or use her key?

I have never lived here. The key was given me at the height of my parents' optimism about me. I turn it quietly, as if I am a thief.

The living room is deserted but there are enough chairs pushed crooked and little straw bags and discarded jeweled sweaters and jackets for me to see that this is the wrong night. There is a party in the dining room.

It's late; they are up to the Irish coffee, probably, all those balky stomachs bewitched by my parents' unhallowed blend of three kinds of wine that unfold as inevitably as the acts of a play. Sal gets stoned more efficiently.

The room seethes with talk. Always a minimum of three conversations, like crosswinds. I can feel the next few hours, the grit of my cheap unhelpful nastiness, just waiting to get under my fingernails. Yes they are boring. Dr. Weinger and his comparisons of cultures with oral and literate traditions, read Jews are superior to *schwartzes* and other primitives. Anita Carbone, the closest thing to a real Italian even admitted to my parents' high-ceilinged dining room to eat matzoh balls; but the dear has converted for Hy, complete with *instruction*, so she knows more than we do! (the implication that Anita is a sucker). My parents could not have lived on this block a generation sooner than they did; therefore they obsess over their own tolerance, yea their cultivation of diversity, for which they use an unwritten guide to the permissible, updated yearly, a sort of Underground Gourmet of Minority Groups. But you visit them. Silly girl, you don't live with them. . . .

I am standing in the hall, invisible to the diners whose eyesight by now must be dimmed by those floods of white wine alternating with red, like marbled meat. What does an animal feel, trapped between predators? More passion than I feel, I hope, if he intends to save himself. My nose throbs where Sal's knuckle caught it; I keep feeling like I'm going to sneeze. *Can't go forward and you can't go back. The rabbit's waiting fo' the gunny sack.* . . . Where did *that* come from? My lunch hours spent in the children's room at the library: *my* high, knees squeezed under the tiny tables, thumbing through my missed childhood?

I am standing with one hand on the unfamiliar heavy banister—in my old house it was wrought iron, twenty years ago the very latest thing. It is too wide for my hand, like a thick rump. Blind bird, blind bird—the Morris Graves print on the wall looks back at me, its eyes hooded by an inner darkness I love too much, love like an adolescent, its meager feet pigeon-toed, driven together, immovable with the knowledge of its weakness. No I wasn't thinking eloquent thoughts like that, I don't suppose. I was wondering what my mother saw in such a picture—not herself, certainly—and then realizing that it was one of the selections made for her by the Print of the Month Club or whatever it's called, to which she has entrusted her taste. Looking into its mottled feathers, thinking, Jesus, who says birds are weak? Who says the small are always the weak?

While I'm standing there like someone in a museum, dumbly contemplating this expensive bit of sentimentality that thousands of people must own, this little brother in its silvery frame, a woman comes out of the dining room into the hall. She isn't anyone I've ever seen before, tearing into the hors d'oeuvres. She hesitates before the hall closet. "It's at the top of the stairs," I tell her out of the shadows. I too have been here for a dinner or two. She says, "Thanks" and goes around me and up, looking over her shoulder.

But she must have murmured something to my mother when she went back to her whatever, her Cointreau, because mother comes out in a minute, slowly, looking frightened.

"Naomi?" she asks, whispering into the murkiness of that hall that was dark as the cellar.

"Hi." Junior Miss, tossing her hair. "I took a little walk." I was wrong to come; suicide on suicide. I'm beginning to feel myself uncoupling.

"Are you all right?" God, that scrutiny of my face. I don't dare to imagine what my nose might look like but she'd widen her eyes and rake over my face no matter what. What do they expect, needle marks on my eyeballs? I probably look hideous to her, I look bad enough to myself these days. But they go in search of some evidence, always, that I'm beyond the pale, that my problems are made of a special substance they can't understand. Do my emotions come in a little plastic capsule? Is there orange sunshine behind my eyes? Is something dripping down my leg? Am I illegal? Jesus.

My mother is looking at me now with raw eyes and I have this very strange conviction, suddenly, that I am the *nun* in this family. Minus the pride that goes with the pain, of course, but still—my mother looks at me shyly and closes her mouth on all her questions. What does a woman say to her daughter who is lost, to God, from God, it's all the same, behind the secret walls of a convent? A Jewish sister. I am not here to go shopping with her, to talk to her on the phone about the ins and outs and ups and downs of managing our men or basting our chickens or whatever we would be talking about if I were a different daughter. All such a martyred mother can say is, "They treat you well? You are happy?" And "Are we allowed to bring you a little something?" But the mystery of my life can't be approached. Sally Amado as God. He'd love that.

This crazy thought pulls me toward her in a weird kind of sympathy. Lost is lost, how about that? I'm about to giggle, I can see the laughter trailing out of my mouth and down my chin, like English ivy.

"Dear—" My mother, who turned away in the department store. I suppose she knows she has me, whatever it is that's brought me here tonight. "Would you like something to eat?" She is holding one of my cold hands. Cold turkey hands.

I shake my head because the idea of it makes me nauseous. I can see the little pearl onions sunk in coagulated wine-sotted gravy. Mother, he needs a mother, is all I want to say. Help me figure out what I am *doing*. She would write Rose Franzblau for me. She would call my father in. And my Aunt Flo and my Cousin Bennie and his smart Barnard wife. She would assemble us in the "conversation corner" of the living room and ask them all to pitch in and solve my problem since all problems are soluble (except the escape of a daughter, her doom?) if you understand Basic Human Relations, if you have taken a course in them at the New School. If there is anything she will never forgive me for, the one rebellious act that opened the trap door to stoned sin and crooked sex and neglect of family, it was of course walking out on my *psych* exam at college. Math she would have understood, viscerally. But I called down the very gods I scorned and thus my plague-ridden head.

"I think I'll just go sit down a few minutes, Ma," I say, noncommittal. I don't have to insult her cooking, whatever else I may insult. I think I'm smiling but I wouldn't put any money on it. I feel like I'm strung together by threads that pop and snap and my limbs must be dangling. My face is all nose.

"You're sure you're all right?" Well, she's learned: if my nose fell off in my hands, she wouldn't ask about it.

"I don't want to disturb your party." She is wearing a pretty blue dress, an old one. It shows her arms, which have barely changed over the years. That I should change so little. But I feel those arms starting far down in myself, as familiar as my own. Feel the heft and bone and flesh and timid freckles, from way way back to my stroller days, that blue metal stroller with the little colored balls on it to keep me busy, looking up at these same arms, what does a child see of its mother most often but arms and hands, always there at that exact angle, like the struts of the Brooklyn Bridge. Before I knew she could be foolish. Before it mattered, if it ever does. Bone memories like this that keep Sal out of phase with me. Attract, repel, yank us together and apart so that we miss each other's fine, fine distinctions. At least if he could let himself feel *his*. That his childhood was his, like his body, something he lived with, came through alive. And not all bad. The liar. Shame shame and double shame. Let him go into it alone, without me, let him park the politics with me, I would stand outside alone and wait.

Mother has deposited me in the living room like a sick child home from school. The shades lowered, I remember, and her hand on my forehead. I can't go upstairs to my old room, who's in my room now, some kid with pictures of Mick Jagger on my walls? But just as well, if I could go back I'd be undone, she could bury me there forever, I'd rot like Miss Emily beside Sally's corpse. Do I have a fever? She disappears silently to her guests, to tell them, probably, that I've come to pick up a jacket, a pair of shoes, a book.

And some time, whatever time's passing, my father stands in the doorway. His face has always been readable, the best thing about him that there's never much distance between inside and out. (What's so different, he used to ask me, between being polite and being a hypocrite? And my answer, when I got old enough, was always too finely shaded for him.) But I don't

know this expression—a glare of anger? of concern?
He used to get mad at me when he was helpless, like
when I was sick. Once when I had pneumonia, I
remember I was terrified the whole time by his fury,
which I couldn't understand; I guessed it was wrong to
be sick but I couldn't help it, so I cried and coughed
and cried, and that only made him angrier. Or maybe
I just can't read him any more, so deep into my new
languages? His shirt is half out, his hard beer belly that
he's had all my life will not melt for all my mother's
tucking and shoving and sprucing. Or is it the wine
that's erased his eyes for me? He looks as though he's
stopped and found me by accident, fleeing the party in
his shirtsleeves for his own reasons. He is still holding
his napkin.

"Daddy?" I rouse myself a little. I would like him
to come and comfort me, he is large, has shoulders,
and he wastes no words. "You want an excuse to stay
out of there? Come talk to me."

But no. No. Having so few words, he is afraid of
me. That's Mother's department, to try to understand
or reason or share. Especially shame, I suppose. Guilt
and shame and blood and mysterious pains that crest
and ebb: women's work.

He gives me a look of alarm? Disgust? I close my
eyes, blind anyway, only a searing pain between them,
and when I open them he is gone. Even the party, that
itchy quicksand, he's chosen over me; tucking his shirt
in, saying nothing to anyone, not even a glance at my
mother for fear of what he might shout.

The house smells as it always did wherever it was:
furniture polish and peonies, and face powder. Not my
father's cigars, which are banished utterly. Not rice and
beans and rusty cod. I can feel Sal sitting beside me
on the arm of the chair, his leg kicking impatiently,
muttering about the place, how his house at least was
for people, never looked like an art gallery. Something
good to say about it at least. What are the effects of all
this—experimentation? asks my mother, picking up
the idea by its corner like a soiled hanky. Sal, you are
real, no shit, nobody willed you into your brightness.
Where will you go? We go? You are a hot crazy star

doing somersaults, not a cold brilliant hard-edged planet standing fast. I am the hollow space of sky you hang in and burn. Inside me you hurt, you are never polite, never controlled, you dig out a holding place. Pre-meds, pre-laws, pre-engineers, pre-men, pre-me. I was right. Wrong. Stars burn out. We get the news years later. We have a couple of light years left. My house gone though I never loved it anyway, this house the hollow place I never learned from I will go home to you halfway when I wake I pray the Lord my soul to take two for a penny and keep the change. Live voices never escape without   I am more boring and hypocrit-ical than you are   I yawn at my Macy's budget soul   What did the bastard make me do   eating raw-heart. Writers says Sally sitting up like a writer have a monopoly on your attention. Gluttons. Are afraid of conversation. Also pill freaks. Are the same. Afraid of others as themselves. I wish I drove a semi. So go drive one. Too late I'd have to be my brother Mike all balls and butt no vision   Vision? Division. The healthy man never writes but puts an X beside his name   faces his enemies not with words   with claws. I always said scratch or be scratched   Why are you betraying writing is American? Anti-Latin. Writing is whiting. Under the imprimatur COWARD I file you on the new fiction shelf Amado between Amabile and Amazing Amazon at work your stuff (thick white indistinguish-able from some narrow-shouldered Brooklyn college mouse drinking beer screwing a blind date in his house plan's corner because they are democratic and don't allow fraternities) swimming around in me wanting to nail me into a living room like this you think I want an unplayed piano and a magazine rack full of all the *TIME* and *LIFE* and *FORTUNE* I'll never have. They found him snug under a dust jacket fast asleep.

S. Amado's final book before he annihilated himself on a skychart mix of ups, middles, downs, ins, outs, borers like worms, slitherers like snakes, cudgels to his temples, tweezers to his short hairs, he is in his shred-ded backyard looking in the kitchen window where his mother loved him whenever she saw him. Knows when he's had such a thing as wanting the wrong thing for yourself   wanting the right thing for the wrong self   Dr.

Franzblau? THE SATISFACTIONS OF LONELINESS IS DEATH apologize apologize and never again my own kitchen window wherein my mother drinks Postum and my father's late again but will bring the flowers she's taught him respect from the subway stand and wants me safe the streets are teeming with Sally she thinks you're a mugger That's the problem she thinks Sit here, here, my mother says bleeding my years all over, and say a thousand times (then take your jacket, your shoes, your book and go) to your *shagitz* your eyebrow family and Mother you are right absolutely objectively Dear Lord we are not meant to help each other or he me. Keep your sociology where it accrues interest it's between him and me. I should sleep alone, sew myself up, suck all my ten thumbs, shut my mouth on the nasty places it's been. O solitude whence come the stones of which, in the Apocalypse, the city of the King is built O silence the grinding stone wheel in my head this how does he live with this emery rasping smell on sight on touch on noise what does he hear my voice O silence and finally almost sleep

❧

248

❧

INTER-OFFICE

TO: The Mayor
FROM: Sid R.

These are not the promised notes from the Transit Authority meeting—sorry. I will not give them to Gail to type. She shocks and worries and mothers me enough already.

I have a couple of stories to tell you, Mr. Mayor, to drink down with your morning optimism. I am not going nuts, I am not trying to extort more pay or make the evening headlines or any damn thing. It's only that I came to work today, over the beautiful bridge with its purple castles, from the Fourth Largest Fun City in the U.S.A. And I parked my car in its usual towable place, right in the cold shadow of City Hall, and walked down the corridors, turned, walked, turned, walked to my desk, listening to my heels click on the polished floor and they sounded for all the world, Mr. Mayor, like the heels of a significant man: a man who manages, or better. Has an office fairly near your right hand (how things are measured here, of course; leaving aside take-home-after-taxes, literal distance = figurative distance, space = trust). *Likes* his work, considers it basic to change in the city, to things that are real palpable entities to him, like justice and opportunity. Change. (Today the word clanks and jangles, echoes, what does it sound like? Change, chains, chance, chase . . .) Has a more than adequate home life, when he's there long enough, home from this double-time work, to remember everybody's name.

And this morning I am here with my hands shaking, near to shouting with pain at every noise, cracking the way a man truly, cosmically, hung over, no kid stuff, cracks whenever anyone comes within touching distance. Gail took my arm when I came in, probably green, and said, "Sid?" to which I nastily countered, "Gail?" and slammed the door to my inner office. She appears to be holding all calls. Smart girl. (For the mayor's sake or mine?)

I promised you some stories. One: Couple of months ago a neighbor of mine took off. Fellow by the name of Tom. Just split. The day of our street fair where I live, a day I was proud of: the city as it ought to be, the rainbow city. His wife swore to me they had had no fight, nothing had been bothering him that very morning. He had left a strange note alluding to some money that had disappeared from one of the stands at the fair. None of it made sense. Now this particular neighbor of mine, no close friend, was a sort of flamboyant type who called himself a radical because his wife was black, who bitched a lot but didn't do much; who mugged for the camera, as it were. Nobody knew him really, the way you realize you never knew a suicide. But it occurs to me that he was serious under that motley, those bells. I knew him well enough to say he was no thief. I thought he was crazy when he left, but I think I understand him better this morning, or understand how quickly things come together or fall apart, without much warning, and I wish I knew where he went. I comb his children's faces for clues, but they comb mine. I comb the papers for signs. Is he taking evening courses at Columbia? Frequenting massage parlors? Floating belly-up on the Hudson like a perch?

The second story gets us closer to the point. Months ago—four? six? ten, maybe?—I was witness to an open-and-shut case of police brutality. I was on my way home early from work, coming up from the subway. (Dock my pay, I don't remember why.) Up the block is the junior high, a gray wall of a building, a monument to the absolutely uninflected boredom of its architect, and right in front is this kid Wilbert from up my block, getting his arm tied, snapped, broken smack off behind him like a branch, a stick of grass—just like that— and the cop who's applying the pressure is shouting *Kid had a knife! Kid had a knife!* to keep the civilian review freaks off his head. But never fear, there is no

Lone Ranger to ride up for the dirt-brown boy to say, O hold there! What knife? O how? O where? Sheee-it. Instead, the fat cat who stands in the parking lot down on the corner, he's got nothing to do all day but back up cars eighty miles an hour, he joins in shouting and dancing. Yeah, I seen it shining, must be a knife! Maybe they'll make him a deputy sheriff. But he didn't need a knife, not above or below ground anywhere that side of the damn cafeteria. He'd come running out the wrong door of the school at the wrong time and stepped too close to this very edgy cop, who grabbed his shirt as he spun by.

Well, the crowd broke and the cop got Wilbert in the car, none too sweetly, and I kept walking. Down around the corner comes the patrol car headed for the jail, and what do I see in the back but a true comic-book skirmish—you could just about hear the pow! and whack! and see the puffs of pain go up in black rays. Trust me, it's funnier in "Blondie." They could have scooped his brains out in a drinking cup. All the force of these dark-blue shoulders bending over Wilbert, who's invisible, and up front the other cop's driving and I can see his mouth puckered up to whistle.

Well, what could I do but join that battle? I, who have a dim memory of having worked so fervently right here at this cluttered desk to create a civilian review board, trying to love the deformed bastard that got born—that same day I went up to Wilbert's rooming house to find him out on a bail bond, getting his lip, his ear, his chest bathed by his mother, who just kept crying with no letup while we talked. I assume she saves up, waiting for this kind of occasion. He was actually feeling relieved: he knew he could have waited one hell of a long time to get out, and a thousand bucks in his pocket wouldn't have helped him. Luck, his bruises, I don't know what got him home so soon. Sure I convinced him. What's it to him—we file suit, we don't file suit. He doesn't expect to win a damn thing that matters. If he wins this one, then it couldn't have mattered—it's a pretty simple kind of accounting. All he says is, "Ever see a cop on the inside of the House of D?" And expects to go to jail himself.

We brought suit—for me, then. The courts, of course,

tried to bugger us. We sit and sit through postpone-
ments, nonappearances (that maggoty cop is wearing
us down, waiting us out). One time the judge forgot
we were on his calendar; *forgot*, while we sat on slats
outside, and paced and sat some more. Well, I've got
time—no boss but you bossing over me—and he's got
time, God knows, that's the best he's got, all he's
inherited is the damn empty hours of his life. He does
incredible monologues while we sit there twitching.
They shock his churchy mama but they keep me fluid:
dances around, sings "The old *su*preme court of
Brooklyn, the Kings County slave court, *cucaracha*
court, dead-of-night court, and what do who care if we
sit and get covered with cobwebs and snow and shit,
flowers grow out our ears, our eyes fall in, our dicks
fall off, our hearts get cavities and the dentist say pull.
Pull! Who give one creeping crawling bleeding damn?"

So it took forever but I thought of all people I've got
to hang in there, and we WON. The kid was acquitted,
the cop was disciplined. (They probably tickled him to
death.) We made two inches on page 83 of the *Times*.
Me and Wilbert, in that order. He muttered a little
thanks, his mother stopped crying a while. Well, I
didn't do it for his thanks. But then I notice he's crossing the street when he sees me coming. "Hey Wilbert!"
He ducks his head, "Hey man," and edges on past.

Well. Last night we were ripped off. I can't even tell
you the details, they are so gross. I mean it was not
your ordinary daily rip-off, no one is exempt from that,
not on our block, not even professional cop-haters and
pinkos like myself. Our fame only travels so far. No,
this one was surrogate murder. There too, just take my
word for it. Rape and murder. Let me merely say that
the gism on the bodice (is bodice the proper word? I
don't have much occasion) of my wife's best cocktail
dress, so thick it will never dry, was the most delicate
and subtle of the violations.

Imagine them discussing us. I mean, these are the
boys who went to a house on Caspian when the family
was out at a funeral. Hey ster-e-os, man, pow-er tools!
We cream them while they over to the graveyard crying
they honky eyes bloodshot. So what would they say of
the likes of me—Sid Rosenberg, *amicus curiae?* You

think? My man—they say, that four-floor house with
the big gold knocker and that orange tree in a box
shitting oranges big as jawbreakers. Empty the desk
drawers. Cut up the shirts. Pour ink on the rugs. Fuck
the dresses, once, twice. Break glass in the bed. Blood
on the mirrors. Write LAY OFF and HELP and WHO
THE HELL YOU ARE. So much for *amicae* . . .

Because I know who did it and I even know why.
Subtle, it all is, the policers of police, the judgers of
the judges—we all look alike. I know, I know. His
fingerprints are unique. He wanted me to know. This
too is an old story: so says Mrs. Olsen down the way
a few doors, a round and sunny social-working lady
who has devoted all her twenty-hour days to a gallant
paint-chipped youth center around the corner, which
appears to have succeeded over the years chiefly in
training up its kids, in their rinky-dink hats, to steal
her TVs and rob the clubhouse strongbox.

We are ready for welfare, Mr. Mayor. Overnight I
have sprouted an ulcer, my arteries are clogging like
drains. My wife is moving, she tells me, with or without my company. She could have been *in* that dress,
she said, sinking down on the littered bed, covering
her secret parts with stiff hands.

Gail has lost patience only because I won't explain.
She is finally trying to distract me with urgent phone
calls: long distance, transatlantic, you yourself from
down the hall. So I've done half a day's work. The
sanitation men are nearing insurrection. The firemen
(fire-*fighters*—is there something demeaning about being
men? Too unprofessional?) have begun to throw bricks
and bottles *back* and are making bombs in the fire-
house. The district lines for judgeships are redrawn so
that everyone who likes you has disappeared into a
single garbage bag, tied with a twist-em donated by
the governor, and they are on their way, with the watered-
down garbage, to the city dump. To think I desperately
fought to defend this job just this last year from inter-
necine madmen jealous of it, or me, who wanted to sit
here amid this rubble themselves. I remember it, smiling: the chicanery and backbiting, the memos and head
counts and bottomless promises in return for support,
quite ordinary warfare that keeps one in shape, I

suppose, and keeps me sitting here in your funny city with my feet in a backed-up sewer. . . .

And the price of a b.l.t. has gone up to $1.95. Mr. Mayor, I am sitting in this well-upholstered chair dreaming of French Connection roadblocks on the Brooklyn Bridge and Roebling's foot smashed, with what kind of bellow, under a caisson, to make such a royal roadblock possible. What was I doing in 1960 or thereabouts when my friend, barely pubescent but who can come at will—how many times?—on my Doree's yellow dress, was born in some bleak bedroom, his mother shouting her pentecostal prayers? I was running for senior class treasurer, planning a career in world-saving, which has since been Jewed-down, as they say in some circles, to city-saving. Well, if I don't save this one, then it will be some other. Can I be cured of it? Can you? With all my household smashed can I afford a b.l.t.? It's a real question. Grown men who pity themselves to tears are disgusting; the civil service, like the military, would never allow such a display. But I never took that test.

Your Honor, Your Highness, they could do this to you, you know. Were it not for paid security, Gracie Mansion would be trashed. With your wife in that dress. I sound like the synagogues and church basements I go to harangue, South Ozone Park, Mill Basin, Tremont Avenue. I sound like the men who gave me bad dreams, the bozos with the lip who say, Lock them up, they forage on our lawns, they feed on our daughters. But I see the way it is: Only one *macho* at a time, us or them. Them or us. Where was I when my little friend began? He must have hurt his hands, I mean the slug-white cop. While Wilbert slumped maybe thinking, The Lord is my (German) shepherd: I want Him on my leash, the cop was bleeding too, his tender knuckles raked. He didn't know Wilbert's head is stone, layers of scar, old ringed prepubescent tree. . . .

I'm taking the afternoon off, Mr. Mayor. Not quitting, just maybe walking home. Fuck the car, let them tow it, city plates and all. I hope they take it, seventy-five bucks worth. I can't wait to get angry again, it's a state I know better and prefer to abjectness. But meanwhile, yes, these are tears. I'll say to Gail. Why not.

258

QUESTIONNAIRE TO DETERMINE ELIGIBILITY FOR HEAVEN

(WE APOLOGIZE FOR WHAT MAY APPEAR THE INORDINATE LENGTH OF THIS APPLICATION. BUT ADMISSION TO HEAVEN IS IRREVERSIBLE EXCEPT IN EXTREME CASES OF PROVOCATION OR BY PETITIONER'S REQUEST. THUS WE FEEL JUSTIFIED IN AMASSING ALL AVAILABLE EVIDENCE ON YOUR BEHALF. WE BEG YOUR PATIENCE—THIS IS A PROCESS YOU WILL NOT BE ASKED TO REPEAT AND WE DO BELIEVE THE REWARDS FOR YOUR PAINSTAKING ATTENTION WILL BE SUFFICIENT AND SELF-EVIDENT. THANK YOU.)

NAME: June Elizabeth (Slack) Olsen

AGE: 56

ADDRESS: 258 George Street, Brooklyn, N.Y. 11589

PROFESSION: Director, Slocum Hill Community Center. Social Worker without degree. (I like to call myself a professional humanist)

RELIGION, IF ANY: Born Lutheran but attended Episcopalian church after marriage

IF MARRIED, HUSBAND'S/WIFE'S FULL NAME: Stuart Laud Olsen, D.D.

CHILDREN: NAMES, AGES, OCCUPATIONS:

Twins—Virginia Olsen Klein, 32, housewife, mother;
Frederick Douglass Olsen, 32, architect; William E.
Burghardt DuBois Olsen, called Jack, 24, ??? (see
below)

WHY DO YOU THINK YOU MAKE A GOOD
CANDIDATE FOR ADMISSION? (Be brief)

I'll try to come back to this.

WHAT WAS YOUR FIRST AMBITION IN LIFE?
DID YOU ACHIEVE IT, OR ANYTHING THAT
RESEMBLES IT? (PLEASE ANSWER FULLY. USE
MORE PAPER IF YOU NEED TO. DO NOT HURRY.)

I always wanted to be a missionary. I must admit I was
never particularly religious in spite of (because of?)
ministers in the family. But the God part always seemed
the least of what a missionary did. In the bush or
whatever, I knew the main thing would be to stay alive
and to figure out how to prod some kind of human
moderation out of the natives, without insulting their
own customs too much. The missionary is to stay cool
when everyone around him/her is possessed or drunk
on palm wine or generally acting badly (un-Chris-
tianly? destructively?) in a traditional manner. I think
this may have been one of the only jobs I could think
of that a woman could do that would have the excitement of the ambitions my brothers had: policeman,
fireman, cowboy, soldier, etc. (although everyone
laughed at me for it and eventually I decided I wasn't
religious enough to carry it off anyway).

WHO WERE YOUR EARLY INFLUENCES? DID
YOU READ, TALK TO PROFESSIONALS,
PARENTS, TEACHERS, MINISTERS OR OTHER
RELIGIOUS ADVISERS?

I never dreamed about becoming St. Theresa or St.
Joan, they were a little rich for my blood. But—read
about Mary Slessor, a little Scotswoman who lived
in—strode through, quite literally, everyone said!—
the forests of Ibibioland, and did things like save aban-

doned twins (who were said to embody evil and so were stuffed into clay calabashes while their apparently sinful mother was lashed to a nearby tree and had to watch them waste to death). One famous time she threw her own clothes (she was a pale-skinned, frail-shouldered virgin!) right over a case of whiskey that had got to the natives however they got such things, and thus prevented them from pulling the murderous stuff out from under the cover of her own robes because they were reputed to be divine, hence untouchable.

Did not talk to minister about it. He was pompous and full of irrelevant motives; he talked in hymns and didn't listen. I have always liked to talk. My mother and I had a good relationship and I knew she had faith in me: she said I was built like her side of the family and had her life-line, and therefore would be a life-bringer one way or another. I have her confidence too. (Obviously, however, witness my present situation, the length of a life-line turns out to be irrelevant: she lived to seventy-four.)

EDUCATION. DID YOU HAVE AS MUCH AS YOU WANTED? HOW DO YOU FEEL ABOUT IT NOW?

Through college (Smith, my mother's alma mater too). Too much. Books didn't help with my life. I would like to have learned more American history, more of how politics works, and *much more Spanish*.

DO YOU SMOKE? No.

DRINK? Very little. (Wine sometimes, on occasions)

DO YOU THINK WHAT YOU EAT IS IMPORTANT?

Like hygiene, if you don't get carried away. Moderation in all things but commitment. We had a nutritionist on our staff at the Community Center from 1952–54, teaching teen-agers and mothers the basic steps to good nutrition. In spite of what the nutritionist had to say about it, I personally do not sit down to eat, but it's never affected my digestion.

DID YOU EVER ATTEMPT SUICIDE? Too busy!

DO YOU KNOW ANY SUICIDES? WHAT IS YOUR ATTITUDE TOWARD THEM?

(1) Anita Robles, 22, and the mother of 3, in Women's House of Detention, after she was denied bail!! She hung herself. We had a demonstration but nothing has ever happened to the bail scandal in N.Y. (2) A distant cousin, Samuel Slack, shell-shocked in W. W. II. I didn't really know him but from what my parents said, he put himself and his family out of considerable agony. (3) Does failed attempt count? My son Jack, took 30 sleeping pills, 1970 (see below for explanation) but survived after two days of coma.

DO YOU BELIEVE IN FORTUNETELLERS? PREDESTINATION? DIVINE ELECTION?

No fortunetellers. But all my grown life, since marriage to S. L. Olsen, 1941, when his first church took him to slums of Philadelphia (where I went as the most naïve cake-serving wife!), I have seen workings of social predestination: the world-at-large tries to doom people by whole classes, but it is never final, my first credo if I have any. If you maintain a child's, a man's or woman's belief in his own humanity, there is a chance. I have seen countless "unemployables" employed, for example; have helped break up more than a dozen street gangs or, failing that, managed to distract countless fine children from their influence; have watched dozens of teen-age addicts go "straight." Last year the son of a prostitute who had abandoned her four children in one room without food or heat, was a canvasser for George McGovern, and he loved it! Is now looking for job with mayor or Brooklyn Borough president. What do you think of that?

WHAT DO YOU THINK YOU LOOK LIKE TO OTHERS?

Physically or how do you mean?
Physically I am short, round, hair is pepper and salt, teeth a little uneven but smile a lot anyway. Strong-

looking, I think; I used to wonder what I'd have been like had I been willowy and delicate. Not too interested in clothes, especially since I've gained weight. (The girls in the teen-agers' club at the Community Center just gave me a coat for my birthday! Red as a fire engine. Sappy and beautiful!) Convinced beauty has ruined more women that it's made happy—never did think about it much and just as well. (My youngest sister, still in Cincinnati, was ravishing and has spent her life amassing fur coats and silver sets and, of course, husbands.) Other than that I would think I only look colossally busy to people and happy in that. I think my cheeks show it. Long days and little sleep have never tired me out. Need never sleeps.

HAVE YOU EVER BEEN ARRESTED? CONVICTED?

For peace march in Washington Square (1965?), $25 fine. Obstructing something or other outside St. Bartholomew's Church, 1953, acquitted (demonstration on behalf of my husband. See below). Nothing else. Oh, Selma, Alabama, along with everyone else with conscience in America that day. Two nights in jail, paid some kind of bail, was never tried.

I wouldn't have expected the same questions you have to answer to get your driver's license or serve on jury duty. And I would hope the answers to these legalistic questions would not bar some very fine people whose unfortunate birth has almost automatically put them afoul of the law. . . .

YOUR MARRIAGE, IF ANY. (IF MORE THAN ONE, DISCUSS.) DO NOT TRY TO WITHHOLD INFORMATION.

No, only the one. We have been through a lot. My husband is a fine idealistic man who was pilloried by the community all the years as a "nigger-lover." He has gone in and out of fashion and has had trouble holding congregations who always lag behind (thus proving, in fact, how they are in need of a real moral leader like him). He is more a scholar, actually, than a man of the world, he has only done what had to be done, and often abstractly. He is much more abstract and theoretical than I am, for example. He watches my hurrying around and my practical shoes and what he calls my lack of dignity with some amazement. His own shoes are either Italian and thin-soled—a bit of vanity—or house slippers indicating his chief desire: to sit at his desk in the study. But he has never raised a hand to stop me. I have stopped coming to church with him, I must admit, the last ten years, because Sunday morning is a time when—after rough Saturday nights in the neighborhood—I tend to be needed. (Sometimes I feel like the highway patrol cleaning up a fast highway after a bad storm, say, the accidents and the animals that got hit.) I don't think he likes that but he says less and less about it (anything).

DO YOU GO TO CHURCH/SYNAGOGUE/MOSQUE, ETC?

I think I answered that adequately. No. In addition to being especially busy on Sunday mornings I must admit that when I am in church listening to a sermon or even praying, my mind wanders back to its list of things to be done, to the street. Is this so wrong. I feel I am putting into practice the definition of Christian, or Samaritan. I will not be made defensive about it.

AND SEX?

And sex. Like beauty, it has ruined too many.

HAVE YOU EVER WISHED TO DIE AT THE HEIGHT OF THE SEX ACT?

No. (Don't understand question)

HAS YOUR HUSBAND/WIFE EVER BEEN UNFAITHFUL? (ANSWER TO BEST OF YOUR ABILITY) HAVE YOU?

No. I should say, not that I know of. I had some very painful suspicions way back at the beginning of our marriage when we were still in Philadelphia, and he was involved in some complicated dealings with a woman I didn't trust. But I will never know what transpired and the details are all gone by now anyway, so I'm not sure how much it matters: he was a very young and innocent theology student and trying to look back I see I didn't even know him. Now he sometimes shocks young wives on the block and in his congregation with double-entendres. I have seen him pat them in an unfatherly way. This is recent. Like old people who begin to remember their childhoods better than yesterday, he seems to be thinking like a younger and younger man the less he acts like one. Beyond that, I would have trouble imagining anything.

As for me, no I certainly have not. Just what I've needed!

WOMEN: HAVE YOU EVER HAD AN ABORTION? MEN: HAVE YOU EVER MADE A WOMAN (NOT YOUR WIFE) PREGNANT? IF SO, WHAT DID YOU (AND SHE) DO ABOUT IT?

I myself? No! But I am not ashamed to say I have helped many young, and a few not so young, girls to arrange them and have counseled birth control to hundreds where their own mothers and public institutions have failed. There are many areas in which I feel ready to counsel others without doing a thing like it myself. That is what makes protectors for our children.

WHAT IS THE MOST HOLY (OR PROFOUND, ETC.) COMMENT YOU HAVE HEARD ANYONE MAKE IN THE LAST YEAR?

The slogan of some politician (Sargent Shriver?) that people must be able to be what they *can* be. Or that we must help them to be. Also, that Love is like Nursing a baby, the more you give the more you *have* to give.

WHAT IS THE MOST OBSCENE (OR INSULTING) STATEMENT YOU HAVE HEARD ANYONE MAKE IN THE LAST YEAR?

Oh dear. To be perfectly frank I remember being unutterably shocked by some writer speculating *in print* somewhere about whether Madame Binh (the Vietcong's negotiator in Paris, a *beautiful* woman) ever had orgasms. And this was someone presumably on her side of the fray. Also, more than a year ago (more like five) when the mayor of Jackson, Mississippi, or maybe it was the governor (this was reported by my son Fred, who was there) was told the Negroes were starving, he said it was hard to believe because all the ones he knew were fat and shiny. Obscene enough?

DESCRIBE LONELINESS. COMPARE AND CONTRAST WITH OTHER FORMS OF UNHAPPINESS YOU HAVE KNOWN. (THIS ANSWER COUNTS DOUBLE.)

Good Lord! (Excuse me) I don't think I can. I'm not even sure I've experienced exactly what someone else might call loneliness. (I have never thought of it this way before, but it occurs to me that perhaps a lonely person is one who has never discovered whether what she feels *is* what others are feeling? I'll try to think about it a bit (not now) but I rather doubt I believe that: I've never thought every single thing could be talked about, though I may not have let that show . . .)
Well, let me try at least to talk about myself. There was one day that comes immediately to mind. I will describe it as best I can if you will let me take a minute getting to it. You seem to demand a good deal of organization of thought and I frankly—to admit both a strength and a weakness, I think—excel at organization of doing, not thinking. I save steps. I have eight hands, at least, and when I was nursing my twins, I'm sure I had at least eight breasts! But that won't help me right now, will it?
When Stuart lost his churches I was very chagrined, both for him (us) and for the communities whose sense of self-righteousness never even allowed them to know how sinful they could be—exclusionist, I mean segregationist, policies, etc. But those were times when we two were as one, and they also called forth great sympathy from some parts of the community and from

total strangers. Oh, the mass sings outside the dark and barred churchyard when Stuart was fired from St. Bartholomew's, not down south but right here in righteous New York, for "a breach of community traditions and standards," when he invited a black family for membership! The friendship, no matter how opportunistic I am supposed to believe it was, of the grave young communists who gathered around us. That caused problems with the public later, and with every foul committee or government, but we never repudiated their help. Friendship is friendship no matter who gives it, and they were human people. The money sent from unbelievable places like Kansas and New Mexico (because our troubles were very well publicized)—ardent souls there, who must have known real loneliness. No, none of those tortured times was less good than bad, really. And we were busy as a fire brigade.

Well, why was I not more lonely? Maybe like what they're saying about women, I mean Women, these days, I never had the proper sensitivity or consciousness of being lonely. One way or another, I don't even know if this—it's not even an event, quite—will qualify. Times like this were aches from some very deep hole, the way a tooth that is rotted out might make a resounding pain with no apparent bottom. (??) Since you are alone with a toothache, is this loneliness? I am not really good at this kind of introspection. The time I am thinking about was the most ordinary day at the Community Center (Slocum Hill Community Center, 812 De Kuyper Avenue, Brooklyn 11589). It was looking beautiful, I remember; it is just one big room, you know, a store front, and the kids had just painted it all a kind of salmon color which I didn't much like—but they seemed amazingly unanimous for once—they said it jumped, or swung, or something. I was sitting in my impossible little office in back with Emma Pagan, who was sort of my assistant and helped out with odd jobs. Emma was then maybe thirty-five, her skin a little pitted, all of her completely *unused* in those dark jumpers she liked to wear—a slow-moving shy woman I could rely on to get her work done without complaint or embellishment. She was getting ready to go on a pilgrimage to Mexico City—Guadalupe, probably—

with her group of church friends and their priest Señor,
I mean Padre, Felipe, whom I know she had loved for
a good ten years, with the terror only a religious woman
could know. (If you want to talk about loneliness.) She
always brought back color snaps of the whole bunch of
them standing in front of some church, every one of
them in suits, huddled close so they could all get in the
picture, and in the background there were usually peas-
ants coming on their hands and knees. Emma thought
they were truly heroic, the men with blood showing
through their pants knees, old women in shawls being
supported by grandsons at either elbow; I have a feeling she identified with them. Oh Emma . . . So she
was clearing her desk, putting orders for chartered busses
in their envelopes, for Christmas gifts, for floor polish-
ing supplies. The kids out front were coming in from
school—a few truants had burst in a little early and I
was going to go out and have a talk with them. What a
banal day to remember. They were tinkering with the
steel drums; this was just at the beginning of our
successful Trinidad-drum period, when they went around
all over the city winning all the prizes at exhibitions.
(It must have been a good fifteen years after the first
Spanish dancing period, when the gangs broke up just
so the boys and girls could go uptown to the ballrooms.
Whatever Leonard Bernstein and Jerome Robbins
learned they learned from *us*—Ralphie Rodriguez and
the Aguilar brothers and all the others—and the kids
got eighth row center seats at *West Side Story* in return
for showing off their steps!) I was distracted with a
dozen details. Their voices drifted back: *Marie's knocked
up again. Man, what a pegboard! Hey Willie—no,
Robinson—he better not show up, man, I got somepin
for him. I kill the mother. Hey don't let Miz Olsen see
you got that, man.* They sounded so happy—thought-
less, I mean—at that particular moment. All the rot of
their homes, their pasts and futures, was gone from
their raised voices just at any single moment, they were
casual and involved with each other like all the children
of America who were not Black and Spanish. . . .
I was thinking that and I turned and happened to look
out the window onto our perpetually messy little yard.
This was, imagine, before the window had bars on it,

it was a very open place. (Eventually, God knows, we needed bars and locks and almost got a dog. But that's another story.) First of all I saw a raised beer can before I could see who was behind it. I didn't allow beer—another discussion coming up, for which I held out little hope. I hated to use up my voice—I mean their attention to it—on the impossible subjects. ("Oh here come Miz Olsen, put up that thing!") Then I saw the boy, it was Joey Colon, who was always mean and loud-tempered; I can't pretend I didn't have my favorites and least-favorites. He put the can down and fussed with his fly. From a few feet away, he tried to pee into the beer can, splashing all over the top and onto the broken flagstone, since the only holes in the can were those little triangles the church key made. Then Benny Stennis was out there with him. The boys did not like each other. Joey was handsome and just tinged brown, very Latin, with the start of a little mustache. Benny was so black he was blue in certain light. But Benny tried to pee into the can too, his back to me. There was a lot of laughing and cursing. I went back to my desk for a short bout of concentration on the Center's outrageous phone bills—unauthorized calls, New Bedford, Mass., what was that? And Delaware?!

When I looked up again, I must have gasped because Emma stared at me, her mouth open to say something. Benny was crouched down in front of Joey, who had his head back against the brick of the building next door, and his fly still open. As Benny moved his dark head forward and back—he was kneeling right in the puddle they had peed, it made me nauseous, his dungaree knees were all wet—I could hear Joey saying Yeah, yeah, *yeah*. I just gaped. It was very uncool, as the kids would have said. When Joey was finished with his swaying and his agonized smiling and Benny had stood up again (he was so shy, bending over as though he was ashamed to show Joey his face) then Joey saw me. And he came up to the window holding this withered brownish—it looked like a bit of hose-end, a burned-out cigar, I don't know, some useless something—and he held it up right at the window, and waved it at me. It wasn't menacing, there was so little to it, all wrinkled and wobbly with a few damp hairs stuck around

the top. He was laughing, with all his gold fillings
showing. I smiled. *Smiled*, can you imagine? I wanted
to go home and be sick but I didn't dare. Emma couldn't
see the window, thank God. I just felt so terrified and
hurt and helpless . . . to change the inexorable in the
Joey Colons of my life. Benny—well, he was just a
pawn, I don't think he had any real problems that drove
him to such behavior except his desperate need to please.
But Joey. Stuart knew nothing of this kind of thing—I
couldn't even imagine what he would say if I told him.
Perhaps underneath he would feel I deserved to watch
such acts of degradation as a reward for the foolishness
of my devotion to this place. My sons and my daughter
were irrelevant to it in a way; only able, I hoped, to
handle whatever might happen to them in their own
lives.

I don't know what devastated me so. My own irrele-
vance. I was only a little more useful to them than
Emma in all her innocence, or a policeman with all his
rules just made to be broken if you dared. I can feel it
now, exactly the shame and disgust and uselessness I
felt that minute. It was one of the only waves of it that
ever knocked me down. Where were their true lives,
these children?—all in their glands and their organs
which they could not, would not control? Maybe if they
were all castrated and the girls too, in their way, they
might stand a chance of being less unruly and self-
destructive? Maybe they could get down to some kind
of real life. But there are no such bargains to be made.
And it goes on for a long time with them too. I was
thinking of the mothers' group we had every Thursday
morning at the Center—the teen-agers long grown into
adulthood, so many second husbands, endless families
already, and cynicism. Now they needed each other to
talk about toilet training and infidelity and raising money
for Christmas presents. My grown-up chickens, I'd
known them since before they had breasts. Gloria, Ines
and Isabel were sitting the other day while their kids
played all around their chairs. Elbows on the table,
black coffee in the cup, absolutely toothy with anger.
Marie, Marie, Marie is having a baby. So. She had
betrayed them, all of us. What were all the clinics for,
the long talks to overcome the dark ages of the church's

worst teachings, the demonstrations, the free samples—
I brought in a doctor from Flower-Fifth Avenue especially to prescribe some method of *sanity* for all of
them. And they were very good about it now and didn't
have accidents. Their families were going to be more
frugal than their mothers' anyway.

But Marie. Her littlest one is still crawling around on a
splintery floor, the older ones all out at the elbows and
pockets, to everyone's shame but Marie's. We all poured
second cups of coffee. If I could have gone back with
Marie to the very moment—that *instant* when life flew
out of her like a dangerous spark—God, what would I
have done? Hauled her away by the ears and feet and
sat with her under a cool brick wall somewhere, until
she remembered how she was a virgin once, and it
didn't kill her. But useless, useless I am. Always too
late, coming to their lives like a mourner. And Isabel
knew what I was thinking. "Miz Olsen," she said.
"Friends don't do you no good in the end." And I was
thinking, adding to it, just as I had said it this other
afternoon when Joey Colon was having that foul ecstasy
of his in the backyard. *Damn the dark* (even when it's
light) *and men when you can't see their faces*.

So that was one very low period when I almost quit. If
I couldn't remember what all this energy was for, I
might as well sit back and read novels and eat choco-
lates. (Then would I be fat!) But of course something
or other came up—Migdalia Colon's rooming house
burned, in fact. Irony of ironies. And there I was with
blankets and a list of places for them all to go, where
people would take them in. Even my friend Joey, her
youngest son, whom you may be sure I sent to a house
where there was no one to corrupt. There appears to
have been no time when I could have quit and not left
someone in the lurch.

HAVE YOU EVER EXPERIENCED A FEELING
WHICH YOU WOULD CLASSIFY AS DESPAIR?
IN ANSWERING THIS QUESTION, DO NOT BE
INTIMIDATED BY ANYTHING YOU MAY KNOW
ABOUT THE CONDEMNATION BY ANY PARTIC-
ULAR CHURCH OF DESPAIR AS A SIN. YOUR
HONESTY AND OBJECTIVITY IN CONFRONT-

ING YOUR FEELINGS WILL BE MORE HELPFUL
THAN ANY ATTEMPT TO FIND A "CORRECT"
ANSWER.

Well, the above of course. I would have to call that
intense, if fleeting, despair. I don't want to bother with
adolescent maunderings, which I assume every living
creature has had.
Then I will have to talk about my son whom we call
Jack. Maybe I would never have gotten him into
perspective, or felt close to him again as though he
were a boy, if he hadn't pushed things so. I don't
know.
Jack was the baby always, large and athletic and qui-
eter than the twins. Not exactly studious, just less flashy
than his brilliant brother and sister, who were clamo-
rers like me. In fact, thinking back I'm not sure I know
just what he was doing through much of his growing
up. I mean, doing inside his head. He had intense
friendships and baseball pictures on his walls, he
marched in peace parades with us but with the quietest
conviction of all of us, as it turned out. If I gave Jack
an armful of literature to pass out for some political
event or other, he was too shy to stand around on a
street corner and accost strangers, but he would always
manage to show up for the event itself with half a
dozen serious-looking kids from school. They would
come clutching Fanon or Cleaver, and they would,
considering their vast amount of hair and their outrageous clothing, manage to be fairly respectful. When
his older brother went to Mississippi in the wave of the
sixties, Jack was only a teen-ager. I don't know what
he thought really. If he was like the rest of us he was
pleased and proud of Fred, who was living up to his
name now that he had a chance to.
He played a lot of basketball in his rawboned way, all
elbows, and read a lot, and I suppose Stuart and I were
a little busier than we should have been, caught up in
the threads of our own lives, but Jack didn't invite
much companionship from us. I think there must be a
lot of children like this: they seem to do all right without asking much of you, and so it's a vicious circle,
you give less and they ask less still. (I should add that

he had spent his childhood coming along with me, faithful as a dog; he was the mascot of the Community Center—but when he stopped tagging behind me, I admit it guiltily, I barely noticed.) The only other thing I should tell you about Jack at this time was that, as a teen-ager, it must have been when he was a junior and senior at Stuyvesant, he went around with a black girl, Letty, an extraordinary, funny, lovely girl with long legs and expensive clothes. She didn't live in Harlem——I don't remember where she was from, her father was in broadcasting, I think. We thought they might even get married, which would have been fine with us. Anyway, when college started she dropped him flat. We tried to convince Jack that this kind of thing happened often, with new groups of friends and the end of common experiences, but he kept looking at us condescendingly and smiling a certain bitter smile he had begun to cultivate, all the boys at Columbia seemed to have it.

"It's all color," he would say, very matter-of-factly. "Color and color and nothing but color."

Letty was very light-skinned. "Race, you mean," I had to correct him, as though it made any difference.

"We are obsolete," he would mutter back. "The third world is on its way."

I could just see them marching down George Street, everybody I knew brandishing a sword and shield, with Letty at the head, dressed for the revolution by Bonwit Teller. "Not this week, Jack," I'd say.

"Only they deserve to inherit better than all this shit." He would look around the room at the dozens of photographs, family, heroes—an autographed picture of Woody Guthrie, of his own namesake, of King and Kennedy to all of us; the Russian woodcuts, those Tolstoy fairy tales he'd loved as a child; the pewter he'd grown up with, not very grand, I can assure you, nothing to be humiliated by; his own childhood drawing that said in tilting letters, with appropriate illustrations: *work is good. play is good. sleep is good. BUT ICE CREAM IS BETTER!* The shit of his lifetime? I suspected his friends talking through his voice. He went through a very angry period after that.

And then he joined the Weathermen. That is not the

sort of thing for which you get your mother's permission in any event, but wouldn't I have given it to him anyway? For about six months, he and a bunch of friends had lived together on the Lower East Side. How they supported themselves I never want to know. Nor what, precisely, their living arrangements were. I have seen many things in my day but I don't pretend to objectivity where my children are concerned. They were devoting themselves to what he called acts of solidarity with the poor and the oppressed and, of course, the Vietnamese. That may run in the family but Jack's style took some getting used to. He and his friends staged tableaux in the great glass banks—you know the ones, they are clean as clinics, down around Wall Street or up on Fifth Avenue, in all the places they thought of as symbols. They would go in and suddenly drop to their knees like cleaning ladies and spread thick blood on the floor with giant mops of human hair. They would shuffle slowly through the subways wearing dark glasses, tapping the ground in front of them, sometimes with fixed bayonets, sometimes with these absolutely stunning facsimiles of severed limbs. They called their exercises *The Caprichos*, after Goya. (Even though that betrayed their college education . . .) I don't need to tell you that all this seemed a bit much to Stuart and me, not only because it was silly (and because he was arrested a monotonous number of times, once right here in the Hoyt-Schermerhorn station of the IND by a bewildered black policeman who agreed with them that he couldn't name the statute they were violating but who arrested them anyway, just in case) but because it was such a waste of effort and imagination and energy. One family helped in any way, one *child* made more hopeful, one teen-ager persuaded to stay in school, would have been a more useful, if less glamorous, act of solidarity. But Jack looked at me from down a long long distance and called me literal-minded; dismissed all the eleven (known) generations of do-gooders, he called us, who had made this moment possible for him. He thought he had outgrown us.

Then he joined the Weathermen. That is, suddenly showed up, knapsack in hand on his way to meet a ride, to give us the token satisfaction of hearing him say, "You're right. That was a waste of time. We didn't make things worse but it was pure aesthetic game-playing." Now he was going to use weapons: fists, clubs, maybe even guns. He apologized and shook his father's hand. Me he still kissed, looking a little embarrassed.

"Humor me, Jack," I said. "If you've got to give them your support, fine. But don't hurt anyone. No Slack or Olsen ever committed violence."

He snorted. Did it seem so impossible to believe that?

"Remember your grandfather Alexander who wouldn't kick that dog that was attacking him, and it crippled his ankle. How can you forget your heritage?" I expected him to laugh outright because I myself felt I dishonored that heritage merely by having to mention it.

But he was very sober. "A lot has gone down that can't be undone," he explained to us, enunciating clearly, with patience one would use on a five-year-old. "It's right in front of your noses, your noses are *in* it, both of you, but you pretend you can keep them clean no matter what happens. And our heritage has been part of the problem. Who needs a heritage of lily-white noses?"

"Your name is W. E. B. DuBois Olsen, have you forgotten that?"

"So what does that get me? That's a pretty damn cheap way to pay your dues." He was gulping for air. "If I went out to the corner of Atlantic Avenue and hailed a cab, you think he wouldn't stop for me because my name was W. E. B. DuBois Olsen?"

"Well, your father suffered enough for things like that, that you think are so meaningless. You accuse us of being literal-minded!"

"Look, even if he did, even if he really did, what good did it do? Let's not even argue about who did what, just tell me are we getting anywhere? Any direction you want to look at, are things any better for anybody than they were a hundred years ago?"

I was about to tell him he was right to quit college, they hadn't taught him even the first iota of history. Instead Stuart said, "Despair is a sin," which I wish he hadn't. That sort of thing wasn't going to make matters any easier and he looked down, embarrassed, at the red blotter on his desk. (We were having a real family interview in the study and it was absurd, it felt like a stage.)

"But I don't *want* to despair," our son said with all his old earnestness. He was at least *serious*. "If I can find something to do, I won't have to despair."

"I've got plenty for you to do," I said, "any day of the week."

"Oh *Mother*."

When he said that, in the tone of voice I began hearing when the twins were about five and have heard ever since from all my children, I knew my son was still simply a son. If I had said, Jack, go clean up your room, or cut your ridiculous hair, or given any other routine signal that we were of two generations, he'd have breathed out the same pained and impatient "*Mother*." So I reached way up to hug him again, assuring myself this was not going to be as bad as it seemed.

But it was worse. The next time I saw him was in a hospital bed in Chicago, in a deep coma which had just begun to lighten—his fingers twitched every few minutes as though they were sticky and he was trying to get something off them. He had swallowed dozens of pills—a nonviolent suicide, he told me later, without smiling. He had the Slack-Olsen conscience anyway. They had had their day, he and his Weatherman friends who claimed to know which way the wind was blowing. I suppose in Chicago one ought to know that, it could be important. They had been going to high schools to start fights with toughs, mostly working-class white kids, to try to win their trust before they foisted their politics on them—really to prove (to whom, I'd like to know) they were not eggheads. Pardon the word from the Stevenson generation, I can hardly mind being dated, but it seems accurate: the bald, the smooth and white, the breakable, that's what they were self-conscious about. They had of course converted no one, though they had lots of bloody noses and twisted arms.

So one Saturday, in frustration, which they called strategy, they ran amok down Lakeshore Drive. How else to say it, whether my own son was among them or not? If they had stampeded down Atlantic Avenue, down De Kuyper, and bashed in the windows of my center, in *boots*, with *clubs*, not only the boys but the girls— breasts flapping, can't you see it? in army khaki, the girls with their Ivy League B.A.'s, for heaven's sake, Virginia took *posture* classes at Barnard and two years of Latin!—if they had raised their clubs to our windows here, wouldn't I call them amok and insane and worthy of terrible punishment? My God, my good God!

And Jack—had hit a man from behind, at least he thinks he may have, he wasn't entirely sure if it was *this* man, he apparently went after too many to be sure, and the man, some young and brilliant Cook County district attorney or assistant district attorney, was smashed to the ground and had something broken— neck? back? What's the difference?—and is crippled now for life. That's the only detail that matters. Will never walk again. And—Jack is right, I wish I could disagree but he is rigorous at least, still his earnest old self, and he is right: whether it was actually his club or somebody else's that broke that poor innocent young man in *half*, he was responsible. It was his act. It could have been murder. Though who's to say this isn't worse. He was going to be hard to prosecute. At least—the only distinction was a legal one—they had caught no one doing the deed. His admission was purely private. He was an honest judge.

When he finally opened his eyes in his hospital bed, they were full of tears. He had no past, he told me, so quietly I had to put my ear to his mouth. His father was not with me. History would not serve, his own personal memories were dishonored, were slashed, erased. And what kind of future was there? There were no straight roads to walk. He spoke to me as though I might actually understand. I tried to tell him he had the past of his family, at least, that—his father's anger or no—we would never abandon him. But he didn't mean that, I suppose it is a success of sorts for the love we've given him that it hadn't even occurred to him that we would try to leave him alone with himself for punishment. He said it was like standing in a heavy wind, watching everything blow around you, all the

books, the treasures, the architects' plans for all the
futures, and not being able to stretch out a hand to
move, to save a thing. Just standing there wanting to
be a tree or a rock or at best a mangy dog who owned
nothing and owed nothing. He even wished he were
the man he had broken and paralyzed that day; then no
one would ever expect anything of him again. Maybe
I did him a favor, he murmured, maybe I saved his
honor. And now, I had to ask him? If he went anywhere
now, he said, it would only be for shelter. The options
were finished, run through, exploded. Now, in fact, to
be precise, the army would probably come to get him,
if they still wanted him. So he'd have to run away.

"Is it really true," he asked me, pushing endless
hair off his pale forehead, "that now I've got to wait
for *my son* to figure out what to do?" I had never heard
him talk from such a cliff, from high above his lifetime, it was not the way young men spoke, nor the way
I had ever spoken. It was utterly unreal to me.
And I was supposed to answer, "Oh there *are* no new
ideas, Jack, that's what I've been trying to tell you"—
and feel smug because my lifetime, all my adrenalin,
has been given in that belief and so, yes, he was right,
I'd kept my nose clean. But I could say nothing at all
that would not dishonor and reduce both of us. My life
was not his life. Had I ever thought it was? He looked
at me patiently, with all the time in the world, but for
once I had nothing to say.

COMMENTS ON YOUR MANNER OF DEATH.
WOULD YOU HAVE CHOSEN ANOTHER MEANS?

Is that meant to amuse? I would have chosen none at
all, thank you. I am a young woman when it comes to
output, I had another twenty years left in me. We were
building a new multipurpose center—old people, day
care, evening and technical classes, home ec.—everything under one roof! Jack's wife is expecting a baby
any minute. Is that the time for me to get a dirty needle
in my finger and have it—what a comedy!—turn into
a fatal illness, like a common addict, like that what's
her name's Ismael who died in the same disgusting

hospital? (which, incidentally, is so dirty and full of disrespect that if I only could, I would launch a campaign to have it either closed or reformed). I feel like someone innocent who's been framed.

WHICH OF THE FOLLOWING BEST DESCRIBES YOUR FEELINGS ABOUT YOUR DEATH? (YOU MAY CHECK MORE THAN ONE)

SAD ☐ HAPPY ☐ RESIGNED ☐
FRIGHTENED ☐ RELIEVED ☐
FULFILLED ☐ OTHER (PLEASE DESCRIBE) ☐

WOULD YOU CALL DYING THE ABSENCE OF LIFE? THE ATTAINMENT OF A LIFELONG GOAL? IS ANY OTHER PHRASE MORE FITTING?

No. Maybe the thievery of life. I was never mugged in my lifetime, by good fortune, but I think this must be just what it feels like: You are walking around, your mind all involved a mile away, and you are grabbed brutally from behind by hands you never really see, and you are robbed bare and dumped in the road. And talking about attaining lifelong goals, one of the things I could always see for myself was a serene old age, after many many years lived fully—not a grand old dame in a brocade chair, but like an old Italian woman I once knew who told me she wanted to go back to the Umbrian hills to die because there she could look out on the orchard full of the trees she had helped to plant when she was young and know they were full of sweet fruit now, and always would be.

WHAT HAVE YOU LEFT UNDONE? (BE SPECIFIC)

Oh come now. Everything. Virtually everything is left to do, or do again, from putting up the Center Christmas tree to getting my teeth fixed to being a poll watcher in the district election to getting the cell population reduced up at the House of Detention before they have another riot and really kill some people this time. Just WAKING UP TOMORROW MORNING. What kind of a question is that at a time like this? It is in terrible taste, if I may say so. I love a thousand people and they love me. All right? Do I need to shed my modesty too? They would sign a petition if they could. I just think there are certain people in the community that do very little to make a salutary contribution; whose side are you on that you had to choose me and in my absence leave some very unprotected people all around? I am not trying to be selfish, only practical about the implications.

My friends were sweet and came to the hospital in droves, except for the children who—I remember from way back, having my own babies—weren't allowed up, and I missed them terribly from the very first day. And already it was different, the taste of the air had changed: my friends bringing presents stiffly, not knowing what to say to me, the older kids all hushed up and uncomfortable. The funeral couldn't have been any worse, could it? I wish I'd been hit by a car and done with it all in a minute. I suppose they only knew me on my feet with my round bottom disappearing down the street. Or they must have known before I did that I wasn't coming home from this colossally dumb bungled business. Some of them were terribly sweet and you should put down high marks for them accordingly in whatever ledger you keep. The clergymen Stuart brought were, as usual, no help at all, they only scared me with that let's-get-the-last-rites-over-with look in their eyes. But John MacDonald from right next door, whose wife, that beautiful woman, was in that ghastly accident and still can't bend a single knuckle, from what I hear—he is used to bedsides and silence. He upset me terribly because I began to think of that poor attorney my Jack damaged so cruelly in Chicago, I wonder how he is doing, and I wanted to tell John it wasn't his fault I looked so suddenly harrowed when he came in. But I didn't know how. So he just took my hand and sat there without one word. He knows how to yield himself up to moments that brim over; losing half his life has not undone him. Any sixteen-year-old who wants to tell me the old traditions of civility are dead, or ought to be, should meet a man like that. And the third world or the eighth or the thousandth doesn't have a corner on suffering just yet.

Molly Dugan and poor Clarette came with funny stories and one of those little cube puzzles that I've never had patience for—they are downright sadistic. Then Ines and Gloria came, laughing and flirting with the interns, and left me a copy of *The Love Machine*. Oh my! I have not been sick one day since I had that abscessed breast with Fred and Virginia thirty-two years ago, and that was only for a day or two. I still do not *accept* this, it is a mistake, not possible. Stuart can pray in his mutter and his robes all he likes but I think this may be more to the point: I beg you to double-check your records and, if nothing else, to remember it is getting close to Christmas, and to think of the children.

OTHER REMARKS. ADDITIONAL INFORMATION YOU THINK MIGHT BE USEFUL.

1) If there is any form of representative participation here (assuming I'm admitted) I intend to become actively involved, in order to prevent future grotesque miscarriages of justice like my own case.

2) I would like to know as promptly as possible if and how reunions are possible. Much of my family, not to mention friends, has preceded me, and I am virtually certain they are here, though I expect I will not even know some of their faces.

3) Some wit or other—one of the young interns or residents or somebody, I stopped looking at them past a certain point, when tiredness got to me—said something about how the poet R. M. Rilke died of having pricked his finger on a rose. I don't suppose he should have said the bad word death in my presence, it's probably against hospital regulations. ("Sh! Here come Miz Olsen!") But I was glad to know it, it's not the kind of information I tend to have at my fingertips. How perfect for a poet. If Stuart is right about my dignity, then it's also perfect that I got a splinter rummaging for a dump truck under the toy shelf at the Center and tried to take it out with a needle from Emma's sewing box. Usually we use those for emergencies like snagged britches and the popped sweater seams of girls suddenly

getting their bosoms, but the doctor in the emergency room when I came that night with my festering infection, furious that I hadn't taken time to sterilize it, said probably one of the teenagers had used that needle to prick a pimple.

Oh Rilke, all the roses wasting in my garden!

4) One last thing you should know, by the way, though it's probably too late. In my absence, the balance is going to shift on the board of the Federated Local Housing Committee. The vote has been very tenuously balanced till now in favor of applying for funds for low income, subsidized building, though I wouldn't expect you to follow such things. Now watch: Middle income projects, even *upper* middle what with the new Slocum Hill boom, are going to go right up—right down George Street just three blocks from my house they are standing ready with bulldozers this very minute. And my friends the poor, these jungle-dwellers, are going to have to move one more step backward into the most merciless of ghettos that await them like an animal its prey. I am no prophet but you had better believe me. All these effects don't take place overnight, of course, but in a while, for the want of my single swing vote, you will find yourself processing more applications for this place than you'll know what to do with. You'll probably have to start turning people down—perfectly law-abiding citizens and their properly baptized children—and when they are rejected yet again, even in death, and touch hell-fire with their toes, don't think they won't cry out your name.

251

(basement)

GOLD

One morning Luz went up the steps out of her dark house to be alone. Her parents were nattering at each other, Mama, Ines, chiding Papi for not being *macho*, Papi turning around with his hand raised the way he tried to scare her, her brothers, the dogs. He could not manage to find a place to borrow money, something like that. Ma had been sick with that festering hand, she was a scary kind of yellow, her eyes bulging like milky marbles, and Luz thought she might die and be taken to some strange place to get bled.

Luz had wakened to find long blue shadows on the walls, and the sound of raw voices aching in her ears. It was Saturday and everybody was home from school; the house was heavy with feet and anger. She ate alone, her head down, her braids lumpy because she couldn't really do them herself, and went outside as though her mother was sending her to Anthony's for a quart of milk. That boy Christopher was lurking around his stoop just waiting for her, to trip her or back her against a tree, but his father was sitting right behind him pretending to read the paper, watching. She pulled herself as thin as she could and got past them, her heart leaping.

Around the corner the sidewalk got bumpy, and the street was cobbled. Ma said it was going to fall in the next time anybody moved in and asked for a telephone. She pictured the cars all collapsed on each other in the middle of a hole, like after an earthquake, steaming, the pipes and weeds and stringy wires all hugging, a whole other world down there. Maybe it would start again like plants growing. She felt very grown-up, pretending she had a destination. She barely looked at the buildings and the cans still heaped waiting for the garbage men, who took their time, Saturdays.

She waited at the big street behind some people she recognized as neighbors, who would be surprised to see her out on her own, but they didn't turn around. She crossed with them. Watching Mrs. Something, Papi always called them "The Jews," she felt a wave of absolute certainty of what it would feel like to be that grown-up with things sticking out in front and in back with a tight belt in between, giving her hand to one child on each side and crossing the street without being scared. Paco was almost that big, he went everywhere alone, and the only problem was Ma would start to worry if he was out at night. She thought she would feel heavy when she was grown up, with all those new parts to her body; that was why women didn't run like she did, everything about them, their legs, their stomachs, got thick and slow. Ma's behind had ripples in it, like meat, and along her belly-button. She said, "You did a little of that," but Luz couldn't see how, not with her short nails.

When she was big, say, seventeen, she would live in one of those fixed-up houses and paint it yellow or pink and have one of those little lamps outside that burned all day long, a soft flame. And shutters on her windows, and geraniums, one for everything she owned or commanded: a horse, a servant, a flower garden. Her husband would not have to borrow money; people would come to him to borrow it. The house would be papered in red silk, like one she saw that time she got to go on the House Tour, when Faye was a Hostess and stood in the door of some dining room that had walls like a castle and a chandelier full of fake candles that burned without flickering. Faye just had to stand there with a badge on and answer a few questions about how the walls were knocked out on purpose and something happened to the beams, but mostly watch to see that nobody took anything off the tables and put it in their pocket.

She was up at the crooked square with benches and pigeons, across from the movies. People were churning around so fast, knocking each other's shoulders and going right on talking to each other, it was harder to feel grown-up, or want to be. Would her face get like

these, later? Narrowed lips, everybody going straight
ahead like they were machines with a button you push.
Everybody looked like they were doing sums or solving
puzzles, or were going where they didn't want to go.
A cop car was stopped across the street, crooked, with
a little crowd, and it turned around and sped off toward
the jail that was only down a few blocks. It passed her
right by and she looked in the back and saw two huge
silvery dogs putting their faces to the windows.

She was walking slowly, dreaming of how Faye, who
was almost as big as Paco, had such soft skin in the
window light of their room—a milky color much lighter
than hers, with the endless feeling of dampness under
the skin, her long thighs disappearing into the elastic
of her underpants—when she saw Paco heading toward
her with his friend Dennis. She hurried to the side of
the nearest building and huddled there, her face to the
wall, till Paco went by, knocking Dennis in the arm a
couple of times with a loose fist. Inside the wall, on
the other side, there were little murmurings, almost
like in her stomach when she was hungry. A dull
squeaking and grinding, then more whispery noises
like water, like a spinning wheel she saw on TV one
time. It was the bank. The big one with pillars and a
dome like where Washington and everybody on the
news lived, where the whole world's money started.
She put her ear back to it, hands high on the cool wall
the way she slept on hot nights, elbows on her pillow.
It was the gold! And the dollars getting those green
pictures drawn on them. She could hear the soft voices
of the money back there, fresh from being born. She
wanted to answer, call to it, beg it to let her in. She
would put a few leavings in her skirt, parts nobody
wanted, like the outer leaves of vegetables Anthony
threw away at the store: she would take it home and
her Ma and Papi would laugh. But the dim voices ground
on patiently, in secret, and she turned back the other
way toward A & S to look at the windows full of
clothes and statues and maybe some flowers or trees.
Once in a while they even had live animals.

She crossed the street when the people crossed,
without bothering to check the light. No one was going
to run into a dozen mothers pulling their kids, running

with shopping bags bouncing against their thighs, and ice-cream cones and all. She walked right up against the shopwindows, all those shoes and sandals and bedspreads with her reflection here and there floating to the surface the way it did when she went to the beach and looked into the water. She started, suddenly, seeing her face clear, and her own yellow dress looking back at her out of a tall mirror; the first second she thought it was a friend from school. Those men were out in their ties and hats dressed up for some dance, and they were dancing too, sort of, waving a newspaper, shouting, "Check it out! Brother Elijah says it here!" They stopped to talk to girls with big eyes who smiled at them—"Sister, don't pass us by!"—and their feet kept moving around in a little circle like boxers on TV. One of them took a dime, flipped it, put it in his pocket.

What was that about the gold, she was thinking again, and bumped into a boy about her size who looked at her as though she was scary. Junior told her one day when they were out on the stoop far enough away from the garbage cans to be able to smell the air, and it was full of that strange—not quite a smell, almost a feeling, better than flowers or perfume, more like endless, black, deep mountains of salt. And damp. More salt than Coney Island ever had. And Junior told her how he read a story in a book at school and it didn't make much sense but he thought it must be true, and she did too. Somewhere, the book said, the streets are water and salt, the houses are water and salt, the people are water and salt—she was thinking about George Street, seeing it turn all white and crystal when the sun comes out—and an old green island, real as Manhattan over on the far side of the bridge, is lost forever with all its gold and silver still heavy on it.

❦

241 (2nd floor)/

567

❦

TURF

One Saturday morning while Gloria and the kids were at the A & P—the one in Brooklyn Heights where the prices were lower—Ralph went over to the new house to take some measurements for wall board. He pushed the parlor-floor door open, noting to himself that the knob needed tightening, and switched on the inside light. Something peculiar: there were three bold red marks, diagonals, on the doorjamb that hadn't been there before. He had met a new couple, just married, that lived down the block on the other side of the Pachecos, and they had this silvery thing they called a "mezuzah" hanging in their doorway in the exact same spot. They said it brought luck, like a Jewish *sebbacho*, he guessed, good luck coming over the threshold. These three red marks could have been paint but their thinness made him think of blood. You could see the blistered gray paint through them.

He closed the outside door and stepped in. The rubble on this floor was disheartening, he could feel Gloria's fresh disappointment every time they walked into it. Was this really what everybody's dream house looked like for the first six months? When it was done, he had to keep promising her, it would be a picture out of her favorite magazine: a porcelain fish flying over the mantel giving off glints from his fins. A huge mirror with a gold frame. Maybe a bear rug. But there was going to be so much work for both of them, just sheer back-breaking boring bending, scraping, scouring. A hundred bucks in Spic 'n Span before they could think of things like paint or draperies, mixing, matching the colors, the kind of thing she liked.

As for the other floors. He could hear them now, *seven* children. The Pope's little bastards. Christ, if it had been two, three even, some human number out of the twentieth century, the Western world, he could have entertained the idea of having them stay, at least till they were ready to deal with the fourth floor, the guest rooms. But seven kids. And how many men? How many junkies among the kids, some of them teenagers, there were sure to be those kinds of problems, who knew that better than he did? They had seen a couple of the younger kids who looked a little like Gloria's cousins in South Jamaica, the Indian slant, eyes looking at you levelly over high cheekbones. Pretty kids. By the half-dozen.

The other problem was that the family—Cuevas, it was—had to use their stairway, of course, two flights of it. Ralph stood at the bottom now, looking up into a darkness he owned. These were houses for single families, coming slowly back to their old dignity; all the rats getting smoked off the ship one by one. Impossible. If the family had lived in the basement, with their own entrance, it might have been a different story. (Though where would the kitchen go? Gloria wanted to know, preparing to be petulant and sulk. The basement was going to be the way she'd been seeing it for years, with a playroom in front and a round dining-room table, a chandelier over it made of cut-glass electric candles, with a dimmer. Only the top floor was dispensable. If that.) But strangers would troop down their stairs to get to the parlor-floor door, right past their bedroom, through the first real space and privacy they'd ever had. Listening at the door? It's bad enough to have your own kids down the hall. For $98.50 a month? Mm-mn, said Gloria. Mm-mn, Ralph agreed, looking firm but obviously disturbed. "$98.50 buys a lot of nails," he mumbled. But she was right: they were not running a boardinghouse.

But—long after all the others, the SRO's, had scraped their few belongings into bags and cartons and gone, the Cuevas family would not leave. The owner of the rooming house, having served notice, was long gone, cash in hand. The realty company, having served notice and threatened court action, was no longer involved.

They, this Pacone, had put the squeeze on him, Ralph
knew that; had probably even invented the competition
for the house, supposedly some hard-breathing returned-
from-sunny-Florida family just itching to get resettled
in a "Genuine Urban Situation With A Future." They,
like Ralph, couldn't afford to buy into a settled block,
a block already on the map, like his rented part of
George Street down in the low numbers. But this . . .
They were not going to have mortgage problems either,
these Eisens, Pacone had hinted, widening his eyes,
which swam with innuendo. Rat bastard guinea drove
a Caddy, just slightly out of date, complained endlessly
about how much money he lost every day, and ran in
and out of houses, checked in at his wood-paneled
store-front office (called Reality Realty; it advertised
chiefly in the *Village Voice*), all of it on the coldest
days of the year, in an unbuttoned cardigan sweater—
it somehow made all this turf his, the houses just odd
and casual extensions of his office. Ralph knew the
mother had pulled one on him, leaving him with this
Cuevas situation. But the house was a good deal, even
if he was a sucker. That's the way you had to look at
it, everybody said so: the house, the *town* house, had
a solid real existence of its own that needed respecting,
and in five years there'd be no touching this block.
George Street had a past and a future, every block of
it. With or without his deal. It was realer than he was
and anybody who got a piece of it was damn lucky.

They had seen Mrs. Cuevas only twice. The woman
wouldn't talk to them and she kept her children penned
up behind her. She had stood on the steps one time and
looked down at them silently, then retreated without so
much as a footfall. And then they got a look at her
again, in her big front room—it was one of two that
were connected with a little closet littered with what
seemed to be ripped crib mattresses—when Pacone
was showing them the whole place, demonstrating the
essential solidity of the ceilings. ("Don't look down,"
he kept telling them so that they wouldn't see the abused
floors, "look up! Think 'Up!' That's where the beauty
of these old houses is.") Gloria had tried to talk to her
a little—how many kids, do they go to this school or
that?—but the woman, who was either not as old as

she looked at first or a great deal older, had just stood
with a buttonless black sweater pulled tight under crossed
arms.

Ralph had thought, *Habla español*, dummy, but,
angry, wouldn't say a word himself. God! She was the
kind of woman he despised. All right for your grandmother in Santurce, Bayamón. O.K. Even his mother,
piss-poor as she'd been, with her four kids on Slocum
Place, sharing the hall john with those Irish pigs and
their three fat bulldogs who crapped in the bathtub—
she had had pride enough for the Queen of England.
Had dressed like a New York woman, no matter how
few changes she had, or how she had to keep sewing
up the same seams over and over again. It was all a
question of whether you ever really believed you were
here or not. Having this house now, working for IBM,
with *training*, in a big rum-colored building on the
other Third Avenue, not the one up the block—and his
brothers and sisters had their versions too, with varia-
tions—that all began with her. But these women, with
those wide dark holes for eyes, indelible brown around
them in circles like two ass-holes, who smelled damp
as the dirt of a garden and made damn sure they never
learned to make American change for a bottle of *leche*
at the supermarket or for the bus—did they do it in
pesos or what? and who kept a house—just like this, it
made his flesh crawl—where nothing made sense,
everything was tangled up, busted, lying on the floor,
flung over chairs. Everything except for the altar and
the dim throbbing half-light of the candles, which stood
in the darkest corner in perfect untouchable order.
Cleaning up the Cuevas floor after they left would be
even worse than downstairs; this was live dirt, eight or
ten people deep, and how much candle wax? They'd
probably find kids in the closets. . . .

"Will thirty days be enough time for you?" he had
asked, feeling generous. This was even before the
mortgage and he knew he could throw in another month,
if they had to.

"Thirty days," the woman had said thickly, not
exactly a question but not an acknowledgment either.
It was a completely toneless echo. *"Treinta?"*

"*Sí*, to get your things together and, you know, get

settled somewhere.'' He had gestured around at the unspeakable gut-spewing mattresses, remembering with the skin of his shoulders nothing quite so putrid over on Slocum Place, a mile at the most, but still able to feel the scrape, sharp as straw, of an uncovered ticking, the cold buttons under his shoulder blades; his brother's scratchy legs against his in the dark.

The woman had simply looked at him, at both of them, a long time with her raccoon eyes, in which recognition seemed to come from far off, reluctantly. Then she had walked away to attend to a yammering baby who was kicking at the wall with her bare feet, sprinkling plaster around like talcum, probably eating the lead, having her brain eaten slowly in turn. She didn't come back.

He had measured half of what he'd come for. Beating the tape aimlessly against one palm, he stood looking out the filthy window onto the little back stoop, picturing where they would put the climbing horse he'd said he could try to make for the kids; the Rosenbergs on George Street had one, hardwood, and it was like a magnet to every passing child. The one old chestnut tree that stood near the back of the littered yard was bare but in the summer it must give shade the way a waterfall gives coolness. Ralph could feel himself settling under it with a beer, his feet up on a lacy white garden chair. Or one of those lounge things with the built-in footrest. He could feel his blood die down after the subway battle home in the middle of July, say, when sweat rots your collar and your shoes are suddenly too small. Strange—something large, hulking, was caught way up in the tree where a nest might be.

He pulled open the balky door, paint-chips scattering, raising a mist of old dust. The ground, where he could find it between broken doors and tire rims, was cement hard. Even when he stood right under the bare tree looking up, he couldn't make out what had been jammed up there. He was too short to reach it, too inhibited to climb up into the branches—he found himself looking all around to see if any of the windows had faces in them. Suddenly he was standing in a bowl, a pit at the bottom of a cavern of eyes. Possible eyes.

Whoever said these backyards were so private? (He had
had visions of lounging around out there on summer
nights naked, like a hippie. He'd only half-believed it
might be possible, but still . . . Too bad.) Ralph would
have been a tree-climber as a kid instead of a fence-
climber, he felt it stabbingly, muscles crimping right
now with expectation and energy, if there had been any
trees worth the effort. So, futile as it would probably
be, timidly he shook the horny trunk, which would not
shake, not an inch, and then pulled on the branch with
one hand, embarrassed. He could barely reach it. But
it gave, finally, waves seemed to pass through it with a
slow throb. The way trees moved—maybe he would
begin to learn that now; maybe the kids would make
themselves a tree house.

Finally, after he'd worked up some force, the strange
thing—a body? a doll?—came loose slowly, heavily,
and landed with a thud, face down. It was a doll all
right, large, handmade, with warped seams, black thread
showing, crudely stuffed, badly painted. It had points
of black plastic excelsior hair and an open mouth, a
black hole. Hollow. It was waiting to be fed, or
screaming. The doll, no baby-doll, had round breasts
unsteadily circled on and dotted, off center, with stone
black nipples—more mouths, wide open—and out of
them was dripping that same bright red blood he had
found on the doorjamb. Huge drops followed each other
down the front like buttons. It had stump arms and
stump legs, they were obviously not to the point. There
was a black triangle painted at the bottom and stuck
into it, the doll skin rippled jaggedly and stuffing poking
out, was—Ralph touched it gingerly but would not pull
it out because it looked as if the whole thing would be
disemboweled right in his hand—some kind of thick
rusty hook, harpooned at an angle and holding fast.
The doll was freshly painted, not flung around and
weathered by the play of eight children. The bloody
buttons were slick as nail polish.

The short hairs on the back of his neck rose. He
stood for a long time, swaying a little, distaste, disgust,
running up and down his spine on mouse's feet. His
comadre did this kind of stuff, Zulma did. She saw
dead people coming up out of the toilet bowl. Worse,

she was forever sneaking into people's houses to gather up bits of them——toenail parings, handwriting samples, wadded tissues full of their colds, anything, it seemed like——to give to the spirits, like a smell to a blood-hound. A wonder she was never arrested for breaking and entering. . . .

His mother had believed only in Jesús, her sweet Jesús who never helped her worth a damn as far as he could see, and later Jude of last resort. But never the black curses, not till the very end when everything that had ever gone in by her eyes or ears came spewing out of her mouth, along with her food and water, and so did a couple of the names of the dead, whom she begged to help her get her revenge on her husband, so long disappeared Ralph had thought naïvely that he should have been nothing but a little pad of scar tissue by now. When she received no evidence that he was hanging by his heels somewhere calling her name, she gave up her spirits without a fight.

He had a dim memory, from when he was six or seven maybe, of Zulma coming to his bed one night while he was still awake. Your father is here, she had murmured in his ear. He needs you because you are also a man. Ralph had sat bolt upright. Look in the closet, she had whispered, he's hiding from your mother, she's got a pot of boiling water for him if she sees his face. But he loves you. Ralph, naked, had tiptoed out of bed, had inched across the cold floor and eased open the closet door. Inside, in cave-dark, were the uneven shoulders of what mismatched clothes they had, boxes on the floor, a woolen jumble on the shelf. "Zulma!" he had cried, disappointed.

"*Bendito!* She's caught him maybe and is boiling his bones for tomorrow's supper. Oh!" She had run off toward the kitchen and after a long time, during which the sounds of bickering floated back to him like a bad smell, he began to shiver and went back to bed. He knew she was crazy. And just as suddenly he knew she had only meant "The spirit of your father, the presence of his soul," that womanish wispy part, not the hard-boned beery father he wanted to brush against. But he had so wanted to see him, he'd have gone with her to more unlikely places still, holding her ringed, horny-skinned hand—she had given him a moment's hope.

Now he could feel his watched head glowing like a hot stone, or the white globe of a bulb. Someone was threatening him and he knew who. But she had the wrong man. He dropped the doll back into the dust. It hit a pink splintered board and turned and lay looking up at him, that mouth shiny, swimming with black blood.

When it was time to go home, he decided he'd better get the damn thing out of there before Gloria or one of the kids found it. The chimneys weren't ready to take fires yet and anyway he'd be damned if he'd grant it so much power that it had to be burned. Walking past the bar on the corner he chucked it into a garbage can, under a lid held on by a chain.

They came back later in the morning with the kids. Gloria, up in the master bedroom with a kerchief around her newly washed hair, called down to him, "Ralphie, what the hell is this?"

He thought she must have found the crazy thing he'd bought her as a surprise, the beautiful lampshade, all white feathers, that was hidden in the closet in a fancy wrapping.

"Is what?" he shouted, resting on his broom. The kids were making a racket in the back, pulling each other around on a board they had hooked up with a rope, enjoying the space.

She was coming down the stairs to him, the loose riding of her teen-ager's breasts still free; after ten years just a little more bounce to the ounce. "On the mantel!" she said in a tone somewhere between outrage and amazement. She was holding a red flannel bag. Inside it was a tight ball of hair stuck with pins and needles, and what looked like bits of bird-feather with sharp quills.

"Smells terrible," he said dully, unsurprised. It was kerosene, maybe ancient whiskey, cut with piss, god knew what. He ought to laugh or be angry, maybe, but instead he felt some inexplicable sense of defeat welling in his chest—for her, Mrs. Cuevas, or for himself as her executioner he didn't know. Shouldn't magic-

makers know enough to see where their magic would
fail?

Gloria leaned her head in her special hollow under
Ralph's shoulder and stood a minute trying to hear him
think. God knows, there was no reassurance in him
these days. The mortgage mess was part of it, it had
undermined him to be hassled by three banks and treated
like a common garden-variety out-of-work P.R. She
had told him he was grinding his teeth in his sleep.
Are you trying to get yourself an executive's ulcer, she
kept asking, or maybe an early heart attack? "Our
people don't get heart attacks," he would tell her. "What
do you have to do with what 'our people' do or don't?"
she'd ask in a tone he bloody well didn't deserve, since
she got to spend the money. "I thought you were a
'company man.' "

He turned the repulsive hair in the palm of his hand,
gently. The kids were too busy to see them standing
there so stupidly; Boomer was making tank noises and
gentle Hilary sounded like she was gunning him down.

Gloria murmured something about her mother out of
his shoulder. Had she been a two-bit sorcerer on the
side? Good Christ. You'd never know it by her daughter. "Is it our hair?"

"Our hair? What are you, crazy? Where would
anybody get our hair?"

She shrugged. "Anyplace."

"And anyway, why?"

She shrugged again. Ralph clicked his teeth and put
the red flannel bag in his pocket as nonchalantly as he
could. But he took it back out again because it stank
so and threw it on the pile of swept debris Gloria was
standing in. Why, he suddenly asked himself, hadn't
he told her about those other things if they were so
powerless? Why did he get the peculiar sinking in his
chest when he thought about the bloody plague mark
on his head?

A little later when Hilary ran her thumb onto a nail,
Ralph felt a little thrill of fulfillment. Something clanged
together, a lock and a key, a door and a jamb. He
wasn't surprised; watching Gloria bandage it with her

half-clean hanky he didn't even ask what had happened
or shout at anybody for making it happen. Boomer was
standing around looking a little frightened but he didn't
care to know why, it was irrelevant.

"Has she had her tetanus booster? I can't remember," Gloria asked as she tugged the knot tight.

He and that bleeding doll had faced each other in the
cold morning air, the cold mirroring air. Had it been
trying to tell him about incidents like this, blood dripping one slow drop at a time, or was the ceiling, the
whole sky, about to rip loose and bury them?

"How the hell am I supposed to know? Do I keep a
record?"

"All right." Her voice was easy to make small.

"Jesus, what, it isn't enough I go out and earn the
fucking money for this place, do I keep the medical
records in my head, newfangled Americano fathers,
you diaper them and wipe their noses and build horses
for them to climb on, the next thing you know your
wife forgets who's their mother."

"I said all right." Gloria wiped Hilary's tears. "Let's
eat some lunch," she said, standing, and brushed the
dust off her white Capri pants. She was looking at him
appraisingly. Did he look as strange as he felt?

The incidents lay curled at the back of his mind,
hidden from daily view like Gloria's feathered
lampshade.

He worked his day in the cool blue light of the office,
resolutely forbidding a single thought of the house across
the threshold of his mind. He might have a flash of
Gloria setting out in the morning, her tan suede boots
picking slowly through the icy patches of George Street,
but he never followed her up across the avenues, through
the rising numbers of the not-quite-rescued block where
their house sat waiting to Appreciate (as the bank men
liked to say). He might even see her down on her
knees, always a clean rag carefully arranged under
them like a place mat, scraping paint off the hearth-
stone in the living room. But she was always alone in
the house, he could feel the quiet of the undisturbed
air high in the vaults of the ceilings, the echo of her
footsteps with nothing to absorb them, the stairs' creak,

and no one upstairs. During the day the Cuevas situation did not exist.

One time, though, he mentioned it to Jim Bean at lunch. (Jim was altogether pleased with him for buying a house; it seemed confirmation of his trust that Ralph meant business, that he was indeed going to be supervisory stuff, after he'd logged a little more experience.) Ralph didn't say, Hey don't touch me, I may be cursed—off to Bellevue, *amigo*. He asked, in the slightly deepened carefully enunciated voice with which he paid for this lunch of cocktails, good rare meat, shiny pastries, if Jim thought a lawyer could help him with an eviction problem that had developed.

"Oh say," Jim had exclaimed enthusiastically in that light tenor voice that forever seemed to be clapping Ralph on the back. "Say, I wouldn't fool with that kind of thing myself. Hand it over to a good man—" He was bearing down on his knife through a piece of gristle. It sounded like he was talking about a wart or a splinter. "Do you have a decent lawyer for this house thing?"

Ralph had shrugged casually. He had Mrs. Olsen's old friend St. James, who did routine closings like his was supposed to be. The shame of his rejection by all those banks before he found one that was content to mortify him by "taking a chance" under a special program in ethnic loans (he'd be a high risk, he told Gloria, if he was the frigging President)—that was not something he was going to share with Jaycee Bean. But since St. James was doing the litigation on the mortgage business (they were suing the shit out of them for discrimination, defamation of character, deprivation of equal this and fair that) Ralph was not about to drag him farther into the slime.

St. James, young, sideburned and "aware," kept trying to "broaden" his anger, get it to apply to more people than himself, to make him give up private shame for public outrage. "It was things like not graduating from John Jay, right? Like having browner skin than I have, man. You didn't see them giving me the runaround when I bought my house and I make less than you do. But, see, St. James is, like, an approved name and Rodríguez isn't, right?"

Ralph thought, Yeah maybe. He had to say yes if he
wanted a suit, you don't get a cat like this St. James to
do you any favors if you're not going to make a big
loud general grievance out of it, get him a medal from
the civil liberties union. But it was also looking young
and quick with a basketball, say, and a natural for bed.
And if Gloria had come to those banks with him and
so much as crossed her legs, the old tired man in
charge wouldn't have waited a second to hate him and
write APPLICATION DENIED on the little blue or
yellow card, and sign his old WASP name.

Now what would St. James have to say about pins
and needles and bloody tidings? *Nada.* "Lawyer's pretty
good," Ralph had muttered. "Average." What would
Bean say?

Still, cheating a little, he put Bean on the side of the
hard-liners, the hawks against the Cuevases in case he
ever needed a quick tally for reassurance.

His days, then, he spent with his computers, undi-
vided, more than ever enjoying his skill at his work,
his talent for order, concentration: the machines weren't
side-tracked by irrelevancies, by anger, by magic. (He
loved to explain their *disinterest* to Gloria, their blink-
ered workhorse beauty. They don't have to like your
face or your politics or your breakfast cereal, was what
he said; just give them the data, the right data is their
food. She could not conceive of any such thing, not
really, but she listened earnestly, eyes on his eyes for
extra light, and then passed it all on to her friends like
a letter he'd sent home from a foreign country.)

And the train was where he did his calculations.
Where, if he got a seat, he used pen and pencil to
prove to himself that, if the curses didn't, the combination of their current rent, the mortgage payments and
the renovation costs was going to kill them. Nothing
less than kill them. By the time he got home he was
sullen. No wonder everybody's marriage got rocky right
about now: Sid Rosenberg had told him they almost
got a divorce when they were putting down the floor-
ing, and he was sure the pains in his chest were angina.
In the middle of the wallboards she went home to her
mother.

He might have talked to Mrs. Olsen about the

Cuevases; just gone around the corner to the Center
and sat down over coffee and *oreos*, if he could catch
her in. But that was the week that Mrs. Olsen died.
Gloria had been to the hospital to cheer her up; she had
seemed tired and a little sad but that was all, they had
had a good laugh together. Mrs. O. had said, Nobody
ever told me Sleeping Beauty's finger got infected, no
wonder she slept a hundred years. Ralph took the
morning off to come to her funeral and found he had
no breath. He stood over the open coffin, holding his
wife tightly by the elbow, and looked down at his old
old friend.

She had come to their wedding, glad for it, knowing
they'd stay good to each other, with a bouquet of six
dozen roses to make sure they believed her blessing;
had kept both their kids, and kept them happy, when
Gloria went into the hospital for a week once. Had
just, for the sake of Jesus, just a *month* ago, sat down
with them and helped them file their discrimination
suit, the kind of thing she loved so much it made her
fair cheeks red. She had known him before Gloria even;
had stood to the side as if to catch him when he ran
with the Padres and had his big and little problems. All
the bail she'd raised, you could buy her a solid gold
monument with it. . . .

When he had led the Padres on sneakered feet up
and down the fences all the way from Columbia Street
to President (where they stopped and the Díos began)
over the rain puddles into the night, their knuckles
bleeding, chains draped over their hands, around their
necks, knives warm in their pockets, what did he want?
She was the only one who ever thought to ask him.
Just *ask* him, not shove her way in once she got her
foot in the door. What? Something, *sí*. The power?
The pleasure of putting his head back to run, feeling
his shoulders loosening after the tension of the fight?
No, you don't fight just so you can stop. So he could
have girls served up to him like rare steak for dinner,
the way little Gloria was, still built the way their son is
built, but eager as a cat in heat, and cherry, cherry. . . .
No. What? You become a lord because it's in you to
be a lord? No reason but the way plants grow to be the
kind of plant they're supposed to: all programmed, no

surprises in the pot. An effort *not* to be. Supervisor of
the Compu-Card Data Processing Unit VII, IBM New
York—soon enough he would be, when Jaycee Bean
moved up—and at a lord's salary. The question shouldn't
be *why?* but *why not?*

There was that Jewish judge one time, Feinberg,
Steinberg, who didn't want to put him in jail—well,
he was too young for jail, by a hair; it would have been
Wiltwyck. He had said, slowly, imperiously, his own
kind of lord sharing the wealth around a little, No, I
haven't any reason better than intuition but after thirty
years on the bench I will dare to trust it and use my
discretion. A strange kind of probation: I would like to
hear from this young man in twenty years, maybe sooner.
It was like a scene in some "Late Show" movie, the
one where everybody cries except the boy and the old
man, whose steely eyes meet and lock. . . . Ralph
kept meaning to write him, if he was still alive, or go
in person, in his velvet-collared overcoat. They would
congratulate each other. Now that he had the house,
maybe they could have him come over some time and
sit by the fireplace; that seemed to be the right place to
put a judge.

To which Gloria had said, I love you too, Ralphie,
but you haven't changed at all, you still got the best
mouth in all South Brooklyn. Those lunches Jim Bean
buys you must be going to your head. And always
called his memories sentimental. Beer-memories. Hearts
and flowers. She sawed over an imaginary violin and
rolled her eyes. You never killed anybody? Pure luck
or maybe you were chicken. What else we got to be
proud of from those days? You bastards gang-banging
Aguilar's little sister out behind the ball-bearing shop,
and you went first? And tenth? And twentieth?

Yeah, he would say, smiling, because she was right
or almost right; if there was more, she was no help
figuring it out with him. Yeah, that's something to be
proud of: three times in an hour or two and couldn't
wait to get on line again. Those were the days.

Mrs. Olsen, in fact, was one of the people who kept
him sentimental about the old scene. She had helped
him forgive himself all the way along. Well, they were
her old days too, that must be why. He knew how many

times he had hurt her deeply by being the baby gang
lord he'd wanted to be, but she had needed him. All
of them, better and worse, had been her life's work.

They had had time for only one talk about the Cuevas
thing. Mrs. Olsen, standing on the corner with her
arms for some reason full of overcoats which she
wouldn't allow him to hold for her, had said soberly,
"Ralphie, can you really put them out?"

Which he had taken to mean *can* you? "Sure—if I
don't the courts will serve them, that's all."

When she sighed, broadly, her whole bosom coming
toward him above her great freight of tweeds and dark
flannels and then falling back, he knew what she'd
meant.

"What do I owe them, Mrs. O? I mean, what can I
do about them just because they happen to *be* there?
Next do I have to invite everybody in off of the streets?"

She had simply, cryptically said, "Those are different questions, aren't they, Ralph?"

Easy for her, with her houseful of Oriental rugs, the
soft lights that shone out every night as if she lived in
a big ship forever at sea. He wouldn't say that. And
she had accepted it. Now that he was grown up and
graduated from her influence, if not from her concern,
she tended to pull her punches. Maybe she thought he
was enough of a success already. Half disappointed,
half relieved, he let her go; she was already standing
in two directions at once, the way only Mrs. Olsen
could do it—if he had claims on her attention at the
moment, so did the recipients of that mysterious haul
of overcoats. He told her to take it easy and they both
laughed, as they always had, at the unlikeliness of that.

Now he looked down at Mrs. O and found it impossible to believe bad blood in her finger could have put
her out like this, pulled all the wires and left nothing
but this pile of chaste yellow lace they had stuffed her
into. For the first time he looked hard at the sloped
mountains of Mrs. O's breasts and, trying to see what
the killer in her really looked like, no finger, the *real*
killer, saw them, saw them clearly, dripping great gouts
of blood; no, saw her mother's milk slowly turning
pink and then finally frank red, and saw her painted
face the face of a doll made up for the occasion of its

funeral. He was too panicky to see, too self-absorbed
to weep. Gloria sagged against him, noisily crying,
beautiful Gloria and Ines beside her, who could simply
weep. It was just then he lost his breath. It felt as
though it had been sucked out of him with a straw, just
whoosh! He thought his chest would cave in, it felt so
empty. Gloria and all that chatter about heart attacks
. . . but he had a different idea. He had it in self-
defense. When he walked into their dusty new house
next time there would be a vial in the middle of the
floor—some kind of bottle or box with eggshells on it
or fishing line or bird shit, any unpredictable thing—
and inside it would look empty but it would contain his
lost breath. He would look for it and take it back.

Coming home from work one night, he could hear from
the hall how Gloria was slamming pots and pans around
the kitchen. Either the kids were getting to her—Boomer,
who was ten, a wicked age, was into some bad shit
with a couple of black kids down the block, Frankie
and somebody, who were using him to run errands; he
would have to be warned again, a little ass-warming—
or . . . He felt his heart constrict wildly as all the
potential of the house's curse spilled free. In the kitchen
her lush face was peaked and tight.

"What?" he asked, putting his hands on her shoulders from behind. She had baked an elaborate cake and
it was nobody's birthday. Bad news.

"What?" and she turned on him, furious, tears
springing down her cheeks; they'd been waiting to fall
for him, hours and hours, all afternoon. "I almost got
raped. Ralphie, these two kids of hers in leather jackets, these hoods, they look like Hell's Angels or something. I came in the front door and they just—like,
they just fell on me. Jumped out of nowhere and put
their hands all over me!"

An old-fashioned feel, he could remember the hot
lurch of mastery as you pressed those breasts and down
to the approximate middle of some skirt until you got
an inch of what you wanted, and hurt her just enough
in the bargain. The kind of boys she used to know all
the way to their bare brown goose-pimpled skin. . . .

"And they said incredible things to me. They hurt

my neck. Mother of God! The children were with me."
She put her hands over her face, ashamed.

"What?" He pulled her head back more roughly
than he'd intended. "Just what exactly did they say?"

"Well, I said I'd call the cops on them"—she wiped
her eyes on the back of her hand—"and they said
they'd—fuck me till my eyes fell out and then they'd
get you and—" Her small head collapsed against his
shoulder. "It all sounds too stupid to repeat. I don't—
you know the kind of thing, I can't even say it. Hilary
heard everything and Boomer just stood there blush-
ing, but I think he actually liked those little freaks."

"Yeah, I'll bet he did. Was anybody else there?" He
could taste bile when he swallowed, more bitter than
ale.

She had taken a small-girl's stance for reporting to
him. She said dutifully, straining to remember it just
right, "No, but one of them said, listen, my mother is
Flora Cuevas, like she was famous or I should have
heard of her, you know? And she can make blood flow
out of your mouth if she wants to. She can turn you
into a stone. Even if you get the cops on her, he said,
even if you chop her into little pieces, she'll burn down
your house and you'll be in it!" Gloria ended on a little
wail, clutching his arm. "She could do that, Ralphie,
it's so easy, I never thought of it. They could burn the
whole house down. Anyone can do that who wants to."

She was pleading with him to tell her it was impossible. Instead he gave her a jerky little peck on the
cheek the way husbands and wives say good-by on
coffee ads—once he had told her, you'll never see me
kissing you like it's just a word, hello, good-by, grapefruit juice, toothpicks, hub caps—and she realized,
suddenly, the rasp of his day's beard still on her mouth,
that there had been things he wasn't telling her. For
every lousy name he had called her in the last couple
of weeks, for every time he had taken her roughly and
desperately, leaving her out of it, or hadn't wanted her
at all, or wanted her and couldn't do it and muttered
that he'd changed his mind, there was some stink in
his nose, some pain in his gut that he hadn't admitted,
let alone complained about. Goddamn *house*.

• • •

He rang the Pachecos' bell. It was dinnertime. *Tanto peor*.

He'd have liked to talk to Chico a little but the man didn't like to be interrupted, he liked Ines's tough cooking hot. He respected that. She was the one who came to the door, peeping out, squinting; her surprise made it hard to see him. "Come on in," she mumbled at him shyly, smiling, always smiling, before he could tell her what he wanted.

Inside, deep in the smell of *bacalao,* in the dark entryway under low-hung pipes, he asked if Chico could come out for a second. She didn't invite him any farther. That would have to be Chico's ground rule; sweet Ines was not a grudge-bearer, she didn't have the shoulders for it. Well, she and Gloria kept up, at least, exactly as before, in the easy jabbering way of women. Their lives weren't interchangeable, but they were all still cut from the same old cloth and had the same kinds of problems. (Chico, when he worked, swept up in a luncheonette; he probably aspired to a time-clock.) Gloria had more money, God knows, and now this house that would separate her by distance multiplied by status—as long as it was still full of bugs, especially when they were going through all that mortgage shit, everybody congratulated them on it. Ines had more kids, more pain, a greater simplicity: she was the only what? native? type of all their old friends Ralphie had gone on liking, with her skirts full and a little too long, with her absolute disdain for the Americano food he and Gloria preferred, with her comfort in Spanish and her amused, uncatty tongue clicking at his adventures up what she called, like an ill-at-ease translation, "the gold ladder to success." But she and Gloria and Marie and the others could still sit down and dig in together. All the Padres' girls—they were still sisters.

Chico came out into the narrow cavern of the hall wiping his mouth with his hand. "Unh?" he asked, unhurried: saying, *Mira!* You don't see me, you don't see Aguilar, maybe at Christmas parties, births, deaths, so what are you doing whistling for me at dinnertime?

"Listen, Chico, I got a little problem. . . ."

"Yeah?" He could care less. *No molestes*. Shit on him, nobody gives you any *credit* on your friendship,

you got to keep paying up, your friends are worse than
A & S.

"Yeah—so, uh. Listen, would you have your, unh,
piece, around these days?" Bastard made him feel like
a little mincing faggot.

"I got it, yeah." He made no move. What do I got
to do, thought Ralph, making fists, do a dance? Crawl?

"Look man, some kids were threatening Gloria and
I want to go scare them, hunh?" He shrugged casually,
like an elbow in the ribs: agreed, you'd do it too, *sí?*

So Chico went to get a little gun. Methodically he
loaded it and then handed it to Ralph, all in the slow
motion of a reluctant man. What he looked like, Ralph
realized, smiling, was a prisoner handing his stuff over
to the cops: that grudging shuffle.

All Chico said as Ralph turned to leave—a sudden
rock huge in his throat like thumbs on his adam's apple,
the kind he suffered when he was a kid and got scolded
or teased—was, "Maybe you spend a little more time
at home here, nobody come and try to make it with
your wife." What the fuck did he know? They looked
at each other eye to eye in the fishy darkness and Ralph
couldn't remember why he had ever been friends with
this jealous shirtsleeve pig, even in the old days.

He didn't have to use his key when he got there. The
outside door was ajar, the inside one wide open. Were
they expecting him? All the lights were on, bare bulbs
glaring, great hollow black shadows tunneling off at
the back of the house.

Mrs. Cuevas was bending, arranging something—
coins?—in the shape of a cross on the rough living-
room floor. In the middle stood a little cold cream jar.

Ralph was exasperated. Certainly there was nothing
frightening about this very scrawny woman with her
old-fashioned high-boned, lowborn face, practicing rusty
magic. "Mrs. Cuevas."

She went on spacing coins without looking up, slid-
ing them across the splinters like poker chips.

"Perdóname." He tried his Spanish, quietly, as though
it were a secret. Let it not fail him. What he told her,
with no preliminaries, was that she had magic and he

had the courts. She had candles and he had jail and fines of money and even powers that could have her children taken from her.

She looked up at him obliquely. *"Tengo los hijos,"* she said. "I have sons."

He turned and saw the two toughs who had gone after Gloria. They looked like he had looked once; Gloria had a bad memory. They had been standing behind him, not breathing. He could be dead.

"Mrs. Cuevas, what do I *owe* you?" He spoke slowly with an air of forbearance almost run out. As he said that, meaning much more, the idea of relocation money occurred to him. Why hadn't he thought of it before? But he dismissed it—you had to be sane to take five hundred dollars and go. "I'm Spanish too, I was born on Slocum Place just up here, in a—" He didn't want to hear from her the same crap Mrs. Olsen had held back: what you owe, what you have, where you came from, where you're going. Only the least comfortable and the most comfortable, apparently, felt inclined to sling around such pious beans. Where was he supposed to *live?* Who else shares their house with a pack of lunatic strangers? Why was he supposed to feel guilty— because he had just narrowly escaped himself? Escape is escape. He had worked hard enough for where he was going. He could be hanging loose now on some corner shooting craps if he didn't mind living with a dozen warm bodies. But, man, nine to five and you don't come home to old ladies and their little *macho* kids hanging hair balls on your door. (Hanging loose? he heard Gloria say. Nobody hangs loose at thirty, honey, not what I call *loose*.)

He was standing with his hands out in front of him, palms up, waiting for an answer he could feel. The gun was inside his belt, hard as somebody else's prick against his leg.

"You take your choice, you choose, you make the thing happen." Mrs. Cuevas spread the unbuttoned front of her loose black dress, or cloak, or robe, wide. This old chick's been watching too many witches on the tube, Ralph thought. It was an unconvincing act. The parted dress was like the opening of a cave, sulphurous; he could actually see motes of dust fly out, and he saw a glimmer of gray flesh, withered like his mother's untouchable skin before she shed it finally and vanished into the hospital frigidaire to sleep forever. The triangle he loved on all women, all human women he'd ever seen, even his mother, his daughter, was gray and shrunken, collapsed under her so that she must sit on it.

"You choose," she said in unbearable Spanish. "Your wife, your son or your daughter."

"What about them? Choose what?" Why was he talking to this mental case? Talking just encouraged her.

"You choose. The house for one of them. You are a spoiled man, you drive a miserable bargain."

"*I* drive?" What was this, a fairy tale? He remembered a jumble of wishes and curses and choices, Beauty and the Beast, Rumpelstiltskin. He wasn't going crazy, the pressures of the house weren't so very bad yet, he didn't feel anywhere near breaking. Unreal, unreal. These confrontations were like flashes of inexplicable pain, of greenish light, like coming into a place with a swampy smell and just as quickly passing out of it. "Baby, who says I'm driving any kind of a bargain?"

"Or you. Of course. You for the house."

It was only the presence of those sons that stopped him from putting his hands on this mad woman's shoulders and lifting her down to the sidewalk. So he continued.

"And what can you do, my wise old lady?" That was in a nasty tone, the tone of the girls at the office chafing at each other. He could do better.

She shrugged. "Oh, things will happen. Do you want to know?"

He nodded, casting his eyes to the heaven of the molding above them.

"Your son will be cut down leaping a back fence. Your daughter will take ten nails in her heart, up through the bottom, and end with a broken bottle stuffed in her for a cork."

Ralph nodded on, smiling. "I think you got the last generation by mistake. Your spirits picked up an old trail." He felt jolly, a little lightheaded suddenly, in the face of her absurdity.

"Your pretty little wife will die bald and wrinkled, screaming your name."

Christ, she could have been talking to his father. Well, maybe to every other man, these days. "And what will happen to me in all this? Don't I get a good one to look forward to?" He felt his toes curling in his shoes, looking for a hold.

"You will watch it all happen, that's all. Right here, from the place where these lines cross, where I am holding a part of you right now." She tapped at the coins with a bare foot and gestured to the cold cream bottle, its pink label faded. His breath, Jesus, was that his breath? He wouldn't let himself think such insane thoughts now, this was *her* trip. "Don't wave that hand at me, you spook," he shouted, his voice raised for the first time. "You don't scare me."

He made a face, impatience crossed with sour contempt, and turned to go. He would simply leave them there like a sick late-morning dream. But as he reached for the doorknob one of the two boys was beside him with his hand over Ralph's. "That little cocktease of yours you got at home," he said confidentially, "we gonna hassle her till she come to us on her knees and do it with her mouth open. You can call the cops but you can't arrest us till *we* do something, right?"

"Right," Ralph said. Sometimes inside the bony rafters of his own skull he sounded like a radio announcer, or somebody on "Bonanza." But the authority in his voice was lost on this kid who, up close, had red pustules like measles inside his nostrils.

"We gonna tickle her till she give it to us free." He winced a smile full of gone teeth. "And even a smart-ass like you can't call the cops for *that*. They'll tell you you don't take good care of your property."

A lord, a lord like he used to be, only pray God this one was nastier. He felt like a sleepwalker facing them in the needling light. This was all the hallucination of an empty stomach. The boy squeezed his arm at the bicep and, startled that it didn't yield, let go. There was still, goddamn it, still only one kind of force. His paper world, its calm and order, its muffled transactions in spools and numbers, had less to do with it than the language of the moon. This was simpler, and democratic. IBM didn't have to pay your way to learn it: it could break your neck or leave its initials on your cheek. Maybe, Ralph thought in a confused flurry, his fingers inching into his overcoat toward Chico's gun— maybe he didn't believe in cutting and bullets any more, violence this side of "Gunsmoke" any more, but it believed in itself. He pulled it out of his belt, his hand shaking, and backed up a step.

They were about to laugh, both of them, but with all the concentration he had ever bent toward anything, he made his hand steady and raised the gun with some of his old élan. When it was level they stopped laughing and backed toward their mother, who stood mute as a stone statue in the middle of the light-washed room.

"A mother ought to tell her sons when to get out of heavy traffic," he said, and made himself smile. In English he said, "Here's where your stinking magic gets you, lady." It was all another scene out of the movie of his life. "Is that all it is, the—" He had to think hard. "The smell of the shit? You do the little music before the show, a couple of bars to get the customers in?" He strained for it; this wasn't his element, but if she thought in Spanish, she'd appreciate the flounces. "The little kisses before the real fucking starts?"

She was muttering curses in a language less and less like Spanish. They stood for a while, locked, quiet.

"You gonna pull the trigger, *meester?*" one of the kids asked, and the other laughed, a whoo-eee, a mocking echo.

"I don't want to pull it." Jesus, what a weakness that must seem to them. To hold a gun shakily but keep your finger still.

"You can't—"

"I said I don't *want* to."

"Even if I dare you?" The kid with the measly nose made a sudden dart with his arms out like a dancer. His black leather creaked with a little popping sound as he flung himself around. If he were shot down right now, he'd fall like Jesus Christ.

Ralph started but he knew he was in control. He still had it, had all of it. Padres don't fall for feints and lures, they get the cards and hold them. What a price-less education. Leveling the gun, he backed to the door, opened it and retreated down the stairs backwards.

Passing the bar at the corner he saw an officer inside, one hand on the bar, talking to the bartender. He made sure the gun was out of sight, went into the warm greased air, mumbled a few words and came back down the block with the cop, talking quietly, his language. Anyone can make a citizen's arrest if nothing else, but it's easier, he knew, when a man in a decent overcoat and a sharp tie showing out, who happens to own a four-story brownstone, turns in a couple of stinking Spanish kids and their cracked mother, naked under her dress.

Snow had begun to fall. It made the sidewalk a spotted hide, like leopard skin. Ralph almost lost his balance once, hurrying, suddenly hungry. Steadying that gun—the gun still real and live after all these years, still faithful if you knew yourself and what you wanted and didn't want . . . He had thought he'd feel exhilarated by his triumph. But it was anticlimactic, all of it. Because they could have killed him first if the old lady had let them? He had the knowledge in his gut just where the bullet would have gone. Because he didn't want to kill them? Because they'd be around again someday—midnight phone calls maybe, letters full of bloody, boring codes for murder and mayhem? He didn't think those kids would be around much, now that they'd lost their precise confidence in the distinc-tions—what we did, what we didn't do—of the law. But the old lady would be around their necks forever. *Qué vida.*

Taking his own steps, finally, he put his feet down hard. They were always twice as slippery as they looked. He'd have to get the gun back to Chico somehow. Slip it in his mailbox? Give it to the mailman? Bake it in a cake?

Gloria was waiting at the door. She had spent an hour running from the kitchen to the window, watching for a spot to thicken out of the erased street. Her small face was pale with terror. When Ralph shouldered the door she fell into his arms, all her weight on him, and he stifled a shout, thinking, somehow, that she'd been hurt. She wept noisy angry tears into his snowy overcoat and, looking straight ahead into the dark stairwell, assuring himself that she was all right, he saw her, dressed in Mrs. Olsen's preposterous yellow lace, in a coffin carved like a great ceremonial boat. Her crying didn't slacken, because he wasn't answering her questions. Then when he tried to talk, he realized, with the first real twist of fear he had felt all evening, that he had lost his breath again.

The
Best Modern Fiction
from
BALLANTINE